THE WAY MAKERS

THE WAY MAKERS
A Journey to Freedom

T.R. FARONII

Columbus, Ohio

The views and opinions expressed in this book are solely those of the author and do not reflect the views or opinions of Gatekeeper Press. Gatekeeper Press is not to be held responsible for and expressly disclaims responsibility of the content herein.

THE WAY MAKERS
A Journey to Freedom

Published by Gatekeeper Press
2167 Stringtown Rd, Suite 109
Columbus, OH 43123-2989
www.GatekeeperPress.com

Copyright © 2022 by T.R. Faronii

All rights reserved. Neither this book, nor any parts within it may be sold or reproduced in any form or by any electronic or mechanical means, including information storage and retrieval systems, without permission in writing from the author. The only exception is by a reviewer, who may quote short excerpts in a review.

Library of Congress Control Number: 2022937575

ISBN (hardcover): 9781662927232
ISBN (paperback): 9781662926037
eISBN: 9781662928055

Contents

1. Leaving Brooklyn 3
2. Upstate 9
3. Off to School 27
4. He's Gone on Ahead 55
5. Back in Time 63
6. Here We Are 79
7. The Discovery 91
8. The Arrival 103
9. The Overseer 107
10. Sunday 113
11. Maroons 123

About the author 135

Acknowledgements 137

1

Leaving Brooklyn

"EVERYBODY," Shirley Mackey began. She looked at each of her children until she was certain she had their attention. "This summer's trip upstate," she continued, her voice barely above a whisper, "… is for keeps."

Rheena and Zachary stared at their mother. Their wide-eyed gaze fixed on hers. Several long seconds passed. Their large brown eyes darted from their mother to each other and back to their mother. Then Rheena tossed back her head and yowled a joy-filled stream of laughter that sliced through the silence. A thick mane of dark curly locks bounced on her shoulders. She scampered on her hands and knees across the half-closed cardboard boxes of blankets, pillows and sheets that littered the living room floor and grabbed her little brother by his shoulders. Shaking him hard, she danced Zachary around the room in a noisy high-stepping circle. Giddy with laughter, they kicked their legs into the air, to the front, to the side, to the back, hopping first on one foot then the other before toppling wildly, arms churning, onto the sofa. Rheena and Zach were thrilled.

"Papa is way too old to live alone." Shirley managed to say between the whoops and hollers that exploded nonstop from her two youngest children. "And his house is … well, we all love that old house and the quiet streets. The Monticello schools are pretty okay," she added.

There was no need to convince these two.

"I can find a job or maybe open my own shop," she continued. "Hoban, I know you have only one more year of high school. But," Shirley hesitated. "… I'm hoping that karate place up there that you like …"

Rheena heard only bits and pieces of the words that spilled nonstop from her mother's mouth.

Life had grown cheerless and unpredictable in the past six months since her and Zachary's father had died. She'd lay awake nights and listened for his footsteps in the hallway. She still watched for the door to open every evening before dinner, listening for his: *"Hey! Yo! Guys!"* even though she knew some gangbanger's recklessly aimed bullet had seen to it that he would never return to them. Their dad never visited with them when they spent summers upstate. Rheena never watched that front door, waiting. Somehow, she knew a permanent trip to a new home would at least make that part better.

Moreover, Rheena reasoned, when they were upstate, Mama always let Zachary skip taking his Adderall. He could run and play as much as he wanted. She let them eat ice cream on weekdays and they sometimes slept late in the mornings. Hoban never made-up stories about where he was going or why he was late. He never got into trouble. And their mother rarely cried. Perhaps living in the country would make other things easier as well. Rheena could not recall being this happy in a very long time.

Of course, this move also meant they would be living in Monticello with their grandfather. Living everyday with the strange old Black man they called Papa. Who spoke with an odd accent, laughed when things were not funny, told stories about enchanted journeys and impossible adventures and insisted: *"It be for troot!"*

Papa's cloudy eyes and empty pant leg sometimes made the tiny hairs stand up on her arms. The brown wooden leg with its clumpy doll foot and rounded toes that he propped against his nightstand or, heaven forbid, his other foot *with no toes at all* made her cringe. Her ignorance of his mellitus condition always kept her just outside his bedroom door where more than once she'd been caught, peeking in at this peculiar old Black man. But, as cringeworthy as those oddities might be, they would be out of noisy, crowded Brooklyn. And Papa's big country house was to be their new home.

Shirley's voice trailed off, pulling Rheena from her reverie. She followed her mother's gaze across the living room to where her older brother Hoban stood amid the clutter of travel boxes and suitcases, quietly shaking his head from side to side. His large brown eyes focused intently on their mother. It didn't take long for Rheena to realize that her 16-year-old brother did not share in her joy. His brow furrowed, head tilted, as if waiting for their mother to deliver the punch line to what he thought was a very bad joke. Shirley Mackey was clearly not joking. She began to outline the plan.

When school ended next week, she told them, they would drive to the mountains as they always did; however, this time, instead of returning to Ralph Avenue at the end of the summer they would live permanently with their daddy's father.

"Summer vacation will be like always," she forced a smile. "Zachary, you get to rip and run off all that excess energy of yours. Then we can register you in the elementary school up there. Rheena you can start in September at the middle school. Hoban …" her smile faltered. "Hon, I know this is your senior year…"

Why does he always have to make things so difficult, Rheena pondered when Hoban dropped the box he held hard onto the floor. Inside the box, books, maybe? The sound made them all jump.

"You call this being fair!" he yelled in his new baritone voice that threatened to betray him. "Mom! This ain't right! You know it ain't right!"

"Hoban."

Their mother's words failed her. Hoban, however, didn't wait long enough to know this. He stomped across the room and stormed out of the apartment. The door slammed with such force the picture there nearly leapt off its hanger. They watched the framed family photograph pendulum violently back and forth before coming to rest at a ridiculously precarious angle.

For an instant Rheena considered which hand gesture Papa would have her make in order to ward off whatever omen this portended. But the thought just as quickly passed. They were getting out of Brooklyn. That was the only thing that mattered to her.

"We can't forget this." She chirped as she retrieved the dangling photograph of her and her brothers, faces smiling at some forgotten comment, frozen forever in time.

She regretted immediately how callous she must have sounded but there was no calling back her words. She handed the picture to their mother noticing for the first time the thin lines etched across Shirley's young face. Rheena knew that her mother didn't have the time or the energy to go outside and call Hoban back or try to reason with him. He was constantly running off. But he always came back before too long. Shirley carefully slid the photo into the cardboard box nearest her feet.

"He'll probably go up to Tarrytown to his father's to let off some steam."

Shirley pressed her fingertips along the edge of the box to secure the container with a broad strip of packing tape.

"Yeah, probably," Rheena assured her.

Hoban was gone for three days. By Monday morning he had returned and without a word fell into the routine of preparing for the trip to upstate New York. Each time his movements through the apartment brought him near Rheena he made a special effort to bump her harder than was necessary as if she were somehow responsible for the changes taking place in their lives.

"Brat!" he muttered anytime they got close together. "Stinker!" she retorted. "Pest!" he mumbled. "So!" was all she could think to say. He was right. She knew she could be a pest. If their eyes met, he glared at her. She in turn poked out her tongue or answered him with a defiant up tilt of her chin.

The week ended. June ended. Saturday rolled around again. It took them four trips each to carry everything down the three flights of stairs. Nothing was left unattended either on the sidewalk or in the emptying apartment. Twice they had to rearrange bags and bodies until everything fit into the hatchback. When all their belongings were crammed in, Rheena and Zachary squeezed into the back seat. Shirley climbed behind the steering wheel and Hoban scrunched into the passenger's seat beside her. Shirley put the vehicle into gear, and they drove off in silence. Rheena took one last look around the Brooklyn neighborhood. The three-story brownstone buildings stood silent vigil as an empty transit bus sneezed through the intersection. A man, head down, walked briskly through a wrought iron gate, clanging the black metal at his heels, signaling to anyone awake that he was home. The others in the car with her did not look back.

Shirley Mackey and her young family rode in silence down Atlantic Avenue and onto the Brooklyn Bridge. Overhead, the decades-old wires and steel beams that suspended the bridge above the Hudson River, slashed crisscross into the rays of early morning sunlight before releasing the car onto the Manhattan side of the river. Nine plus miles later they left the Franklin D. Roosevelt East River Drive and headed toward the George Washington Bridge. Shirley pulled the car over and let Hoban take over the driving. It was the only way she knew how to say that she understood. Things indeed were not fair.

2

Upstate

THEY ARRIVED in Monticello before dusk. Tall stone columns marked the corners of their destination. The giant walnut tree in Papa's front yard came into view as Hoban turned the vehicle onto Clifton Avenue. The enormous gray house with blue shutters dwarfed the six other houses on the street even though it was situated back several dozen yards from the curb. Two long windows were on either side of its front door. Jutting from the slanted roof, two smaller pentagonal shaped windows rested above them. Rheena had drawn pictures of this house countless times. Because rectangles, squares and triangles are easy to draw, they served as the cover art for more than one *My Summer Vacation* back to school report.

The upstairs windows, like squared eyes with triangles for lids, monitored their safe arrival. The rectangle mouth of the front door positioned to exclaim a greeting of excitement and anticipation.

Papa strode out to meet the car as if he had known the exact moment of their arrival. Rheena threaded herself unceremoniously out of the back seat of the vehicle followed by Zachary. She stood at the edge of the driveway and studied the array of wildflowers, the ragged bushes already heavy with summer berries and sparrows and Grosbeaks that darted amongst the branches. A grey squirrel scurried up the black walnut tree to improve its vantage point of its new neighbors. In no time, Zachary was out of the vehicle running and tumbling across the lawn. Papa ambled to the curb as Shirley pulled herself from the passenger's seat to let the old man wrap her into his arms. Rheena and Hoban stood shoulder to elbow, instant allies, examining their new home.

The house was painted a fern meadow blue. Dark cobalt shutters flanked each window, front, back and side. The grey stones that covered the lower portion of the house, the tall chimney in the roof with stones that matched the front of the house made the place look strong and safe.

The house had a porch. Clusters of maidenhair fern took turns with the pink azaleas and bee balm growing along the edge of the porch. A short distance from the side of the house tomatoes and peppers leaned against broomstick poles. Aluminum pie tins slapped lazily against the poles tapping out a rhythm that added to the tranquil soundscape. Clumps of deep purple irises and bright orange daylilies bloomed on their elongated stems throughout the expansive yard. Still, there was plenty of room for play. Already, Zachary was twirling wildly on a tire that hung from a maple tree.

Rheena and Hoban faced their new home, taking in the simple details that had always been there but now wanted more of their attention. The colors, shapes, sounds and smells would soon be a permanent part of their lives. There was no name-calling now. Together they faced their new future. Hoban sighed.

In the upstairs window a light flickered. Rheena's eyes darted up in response to the sudden flash of light. She noted, for an instant, the dark window was lit bright then dark again. She glanced up at her big brother. Hoban frowned, turned his head to glance into the setting sun behind them, then back to the upper room window. *Yes!* She realized he had seen it too, the flicker of light then darkness again. Had they both seen the house mischievously wink at them?

For a fleeting moment, Rheena wondered if living here permanently was such a good idea. She squared her shoulders, looked up at her brother then back at the house. Hoban gently rested his hand on his little sister's shoulder and pulled her close.

Papa folded each of them into his long brown arms as he muttered a complicated greeting. They in turn murmured about the trip up, the fast food stops along the way and how glad they were to have arrived before dark. Papa seemed much older than she remembered him being, Rheena thought as the old man led them inside.

In short order, all the suitcases, bags, boxes and crates they had crammed into the family's hatchback cluttered Papa's living room. Bags of toys and boxes of games were carried to the two of the five upstairs bedrooms. Winter clothes were hung in closets, books squeezed onto already crammed bookshelves, containers of food placed in the kitchen refrigerator and pantry. When all the belongings were carried to their final destinations throughout the house, Papa orchestrated the unpacking.

The storing of the household items, dishes, pots, and pans was left for last. And for a week, Hoban used this as an excuse to fall asleep on the sofa at the end of the day. After a while he made no excuses. When he came home long after everyone else was in bed, he plopped down on the sofa and slept. Within the week Shirley found a part-time job as a hairdresser in a beauty salon in Middletown.

Their summer began to unfold as usual. Most of Shirley's time was spent at work, getting ready for work, or traveling to work. For the others, seasonal friendships were rekindled and that made the first two weeks of the summer feel like most other summer vacations. Rheena, Zachary and Papa fished along the shallow edges of the Beaverkill River, hiked deep in the woods near the reservoir, attended all the parades, festivals and fairs and spent the cool of the evening outside catching and counting fireflies.

Rheena and Zachary had full run of the house, the front and backyard and the neighborhood. The only places off limits when not accompanied by their mother, Hoban or Papa were in town and their grandfather's bedroom.

"Chi'ren kin go inna part da house dey please," Papa told Shirley more than once. When she was alone with the children, however, Shirley admonished them to respect their grandfather's privacy. To Rheena and Zachary, Papa's bedroom, strewn with colorful pieces of cloth, baskets filled with oddly shaped stones, statues carved of wood and ivory became a forbidden sanctum that held countless intriguing mysteries and treasures.

"I don't want you breaking any of his stuff," Shirley warned over their protests. Sometimes Papa allowed them to take a closer look at these things. On these occasions the children moved with their mother about the room fingering the statues that waited like tiny sentinels on his dresser and by his chair. On the dresser were woven baskets that contained fancy buttons of all shapes and sizes and colorful pins identifying elections, rallies, and meetings. There were envelopes and folders, books and magazines stacked in angled piles in every available horizontal space. He had cardboard boxes, cigar boxes, even shoeboxes filled with pamphlets, papers, and photographs. Everywhere they looked was something hanging or resting with a story to tell. And Papa was ever eager to tell it. If anyone touched it, Papa was ready to tell who touched it before them. If they read it, Papa told them who wrote it, when and why.

Beneath his great high back chair Papa kept one special cigar box of treasures. This he didn't want touched.

One balmy summer night, as they wandered about Papa's bedroom touching this item or handling another, Papa plopped down in his chair and joined them. He reached his long arm down beneath the chair and retrieved the TeAmo cigar box that was secreted there. Shirley, Hoban, and Zachary gathered around the chair to get a closer look, while Rheena lingered near the door. Papa raised the well-worn lid of the cigar box, taking care not to tear the strips of cellophane tape that held the lid in place, his long fingers gently tapping and then lifting its content. He thumbed through several stacks of photographs before deciding on the one to entertain his small family with tales centered on the faces that stared at them from places set long ago.

This one, Papa offered, rubbing the tiny image with his fingers, was a cousin or maybe a buddy. Another, the son, or daughter, sometimes the wife of someone whose name he recalled one moment and not the next. Still another photo, only the picture remembered the chubby-faced baby, now grown. Each face, each representation, each image had a story.

"Lemme see!" Zachary pleaded, his hands flapping at his wrist as he bounced up and down beside Papa's chair.

"Careful!" Shirley cautioned gently lowering his arms back down to his side.

From across the room Rheena could see the curls of paper and Papa's long dark fingers that lifted them carefully from their place. The rest of her family were already oohing and aahing at the images when Rheena decided to join the circle. Shirley slipped her arm around Rheena's shoulder.

"Papa says, this one here is your daddy," she said softly. She moved the picture she held between her fingertips closer so that Rheena could get a better look.

"Wer'nt mor'n five, maybe six," Papa offered.

Rheena stared at the likeness of the little brown boy younger than her own brother that Papa was telling them was her father. Of late, she could not even remember what her father looked like. And that bothered her. Now, she feared, the image of this small child, not yet her father, would be fixed in her mind. She did not want that.

Rheena pushed the picture back to her mother. After looking at the picture an instant longer, Shirley in turn placed it gently back into the box balanced on Papa's knees.

"Who are these old-timey people?" Hoban broke the reverie.

"Let me see," intoned Zachary. This time he made a deliberate effort to hold his arms firmly at his side.

Shirley moved from her daughter's side to join the others as they gathered now around Hoban. Heads pressed together, they passed a set of ochre squares of paper between them and then to Papa.

"Ole timey." Papa laughed. "This the Hammond Plantation. These the cullits that worked it," his voice more somber.

"You were born on a plantation?" Hoban asked.

"Na. Not me. But my granddaddy was." Papa answered matter-of-factly. Rheena and Zachary exchanged glances then covered their mouths to stifle their giggles.

"A real plantation?" Zachary asked laughter exploding through his fingers.

"Real as you wanna be," Papa answered. "What's so funny?" he asked.

"Tryna imagine you little … with a granddaddy." Rheena laughed out loud this time.

"Oh, you think I was born a wrinkled old man?"

Everyone laughed enjoying either the thought of Papa as a small child or the possibility that someone was once his granddaddy. They passed the pictures around in silence. It was the picture of a gathering outside a great barn that caught Rheena's interest.

"Who are they, Papa?" she asked stretching her arm toward her grandfather.

In her hand Rheena held five cracking images of people caught in mid-stride. Gardening tools in this one's hand, fishing poles slung over the shoulder of another, a group of men and boys crowded onto a wagon all headed somewhere that their faces said they did not want to go.

Shirley, Hoban, Zachary and Rheena all crowded around Papa's chair as they strained to get a better look. Rheena turned the curled pictures this way and that to get a clearer view of the tiny dots that stared back at them. The tiny sepia square of paper moved from one eager hand to the next until it arrived back to Papa. He stared at it for a while before speaking.

"This one b'fore my time," he told them as he studied the image.

"Look at this!" Hoban offered. "This must be some of your family too, Papa." They all turned to him. "This little girl looks just like Rheena."

All hands reached for the picture at the same time. It was a picture of children by a covered wagon. Two dozen or more small brown faces stared back at them. They stood in three ill-ordered lines, their clothes a hodgepodge of fabric. Some stood tall, some were short. Three little ones sat crossed legged on the ground in front of the rest. And there she was the likeness startling. In the back row, her hair a bushy tangle of braids was the face of an unmistakably distant relative of Rheena Mackey.

"Somebody needs to get her hair done," Shirley joked.

Once again, they all laughed, harder this time, everyone that is except Rheena.

"Gimme that!"

Rheena snatched the photograph from her brother, dropped it with the rest of the pictures back into the box and closed the lid with as close to a slam as she could manage then handed the box back to Papa.

"Silly!" she muttered lifting her chin into the air just a little higher than usual.

Papa leaned back in his chair and closed his eyes. Whenever he leaned back like that, arms folded across his lap, he was either ready to tell a story or ready to fall asleep. He was a wealth of stories. Most of the stories were welcomed and entertaining. It seemed Rheena, however, was the only one that got tired of their telling and retelling.

Now, they all waited politely expecting to hear his snoring. Shirley slipped the box from the old man's lap and slid in back into its place beneath the chair. The room had become stuffy; the windows shut tight against the night chill. There was restlessness in the air that made it near impossible for them to pay any more attention, until Papa opened his eyes and for an uncomfortably long few seconds stared absently at the ceiling. He crossed his long leg over his knee, waved his large, animated hands before he spoke.

"Was a lot what brought us to this place. This place where we at now."

His arms circled the air as if to take in the room, the house, the village, maybe the whole world even. He pointed at Rheena's head and spoke of Madame Walker. He rambled on about Marcus Garvey, Mamie Till, Haile Selassie, and other, what he referred to as *way makers*. In his sing-song voice, he droned on about the great nations of Africa, the motherland, he called it. Papa spoke of the Songhay Empire as if he himself had walked the streets of this ancient African city. With a far-off stare, he described the long stone columns that stood at the entrance to the emperor's palace, the people, attired in flowing garb, hurrying through the streets, the children playing mancala with shiny stones while they waited for their parents at the market. And the rich deposits of precious gems that lay like so many pebbles along the riverbank.

Rheena and her brothers listened respectfully. Zachary stared out the window and watched the evening as it wore on into darkness. Hoban pulled himself away from the others and waited disinterestedly by the bedroom door, while Rheena, pranced around the room examining each artifact. They were ready to get on with another more exciting activity. It was becoming impossible for them to pay attention.

And Rheena could not take her mind off the images in the pictures. Could she actually be related to those dirt-poor people that left their impressions in those photographs? She was ashamed and knew that Hoban would take the next opportunity to laugh at her and her father's ancestors.

"Don't touch that!" Rheena heard Shirley warn their little brother for the third time.

They were all ignoring Papa until he began to speak of the Crossing and of the South.

"Dey come in Africa and stole da peoples," he lamented. "So many peoples. Men, women and chi'ren too. Stripped and beaten! Stolen away from dey home. Pushed inna big boats! Ships, dey was."

The old man's brow furrowed; his eyes welled with tears.

"Dey was solt t' da highest bidder! Like cattle. Like cows and horses dey was solt. An' work harder!" he hissed in anger. "Worse of all," Papa continued, his usual sultry voice raspy now with his rage, "They was hep'ed wit dat treachery! Hep'd by dey own! By dey own!" he repeated for emphasis.

Then he cried.

Tears rolled down the curve of his chiseled brown cheekbone. He made a soft humming sound in his throat that could have been amusing had it not made them feel awkward and uneasy. Shirley rubbed Papa's back as he sobbed quietly. Zachary seemed not to even notice the old man's sadness. Hoban watched uncomfortably in silence.

Rheena felt shame wash over her. The shame for her father being dead; shame of her grandfather crying; and for the dirt-poor people in the photographs. She muttered something about the stories being the silly imaginings of a silly old man as she backed warily toward the door.

She hadn't intended to be rude, but grown people crying was embarrassing. Not to mention, she was still upset about the picture. The likeness to her of that dark bedraggled little slave girl guaranteed the teasing that was sure to come from her older brother, Hoban.

The three of them, her and her two brothers, had all inherited their mother Shirley's soft fine facial features and her determined outspoken personality; however, with different fathers, Hoban had fair skin, she and Zachary had skin the color of chocolate. There was no doubt the two of them descended from Papa's Africa and from his plantation slaves, Rheena reasoned. Hoban on the other hand, she knew, resentment and anger burning in her chest, descended from some place, she was certain, where the people wore real clothes and didn't *wrap themselves in fine fabric.* Someplace where the children didn't *play with precious gems that they found lying on the ground by the riverside while they waited for their parents at the market.* Someplace that didn't get itself enslaved. Even the voice of her thoughts sounded sullen and mocking. Her big brother's people came from someplace that didn't embarrass. And furthermore, Rheena's inner voice taunted: Her Black father was dead. His Spanish father was still alive.

She'd had enough of Papa and his ridiculous box of papers, buttons, and pictures for one night.

Rheena headed toward the bedroom door, but Hoban stepped in the way to block her exit. She tried to shove pass him. He smiled; his face handsome with mischief. He raised one eyebrow and winked his eye. Hoban wobbled his head, then crossed his arms across his chest. The two glanced to see if their mother watched. But she was still comforting Papa, rubbing his shoulder and cooing words of solace into the top of his head.

But before the sibling banter between Rheena and big brother Hoban could escalate beyond a push or two, Zachary interrupted. He pointed to something that until that moment had gone unnoticed.

"Papa! What's under there?" Zachary chirped.

The two-foot-high mound rested beside the dresser. It had been hidden, covered by fabric, amongst the countless other items that cluttered the old man's bedroom.

Zachary slid the mud cloth covering to the floor and revealed an odd shaped, two-foot high, wooden carving. Papa turned to Zachary and in an instant, Papa's emotional display ended.

"Aah! Dat *ewe*!" He said simply as he wiped his tears with his shirt sleeve.

"It looks like a drum," Zachary exclaimed. Rheena shrugged past Hoban in order to get a better look at the object of renewed interest. She too was now drawn from her own conflicted emotions by curiosity.

"Dat *ewe*," their grandfather repeated as he pulled himself up from his chair.

"Is it real?" Hoban joined the circle that formed around the drum. He dismissed the opportunity to tease his baby sister in favor of this new venture. The teen extended his hand in the direction of *ewe* then drew it back, uncertain of making contact with the animal skin surface.

"It be real, tru' 'nuf! It called: *talking drum*," Papa said. His face smudged damp from tears; he smiled a broad toothy smile.

"It's beautiful," Shirley managed to say.

The wood out of which the drum had been carved was still recognizable as a tree. Intricate slashes crisscrossed the surface of the wood. Thongs of leather, which appear to be tendons or some such animal part, stretched from the top of the drum to its tapered middle and held an animal skin taunt in place.

It might have been her imagination, but Rheena was certain she could feel a subtle, palpable sensation emanating from the drum. It seemed to radiate out from the *ewe* until it filed the entire room. A gentle pulse rocked her slowly where she stood, rhythmically like the beginning of a dance that begged to be performed.

"It be a magical t'ing. Bought wit a tur'bel great price," Papa added.

Shirley rubbed her arms hoping to displace the tingling that crept up her spine.

"When da drummer, 'e got some'ting to say, … t'ing dat be bery, bery 'portant, … 'e use *ewe*. Talk o' ewe drum has same message to all peoples."

"How so, Papa?" Hoban asked moving in to stand near his brother and sister.

"'E don' be tawkin' t'da' ear." Papa moved his long boney finger from the side of his head and jabbed it firmly into Rheena's chest. "Ewe talk 'n da' soul language. Dat be how we all kin un'erstan' talkin' drum."

"It sure looks expensive," Rheena said as she absently fingered the spot on her chest that Papa had just touched.

"Dat's ridiculous. Not money! Silly chile!" her grandfather scolded with a dismissive chuckle and a flick of his long fingers.

"I'm not a child." Rheena gritted her teeth and murmured under her breath. "… certainly not a silly one," she thought to herself her chin tipped into the air just in case anyone cared. But everyone's attention was fixed, captivated by the talking drum.

To his enraptured young family Papa explained how, "... many, many years ago, I be a youngster not much older den you boy," he said, indicating Zachary. "I fount da talking drum, dis bery one, hidden in an old cabin down in South Carolina where I be borned."

The sound was imperceptible at first, a distant rumble heard under Papa's singsong voice. Like thunder rolling across the valley, growing louder as it grew closer. Yet, still far away.

Rheena tried to ignore it. She looked around to see if anyone else heard it. Hoban glanced toward the window and frowned. Shirley continued rubbing her arms as if to ward off the cold. But the room was warm, uncomfortably warm.

Rheena wanted to say: *Can you hear that?* But decided not to risk the ridicule. If they did hear the rumbling, then no one let on. Maybe later she would mention it to her mother. Right now, she didn't want anyone else yelling at her, or calling her ridiculous and dismissing her as silly with crazy notions.

The talking drum stood in the corner between the dresser and the wall, inviting, with its silence, someone to come near it. Zachary took a brave step toward the drum. Shirley grabbed him by his arm.

"Can I touch it, Mama?" he whispered.

"I don't know," Shirley whispered.

They looked to Papa; however, he too stared at *ewe*, waiting.

"Well?" said Rheena raising her voice slightly above the rumble that she decided only she heard. "Can he?" No one answered. "Then, can *you* play it, Papa? If you play the ewe, then I'll dance. We can all dance. That would be fun. Right, Mama?" Shirley shrugged.

"No, no." Papa chuckled, his voice breaking into a familiar high chuckle. "Not me. My soul 'bout played out."

The old man moved back to his chair and sat down with a plop. Rheena looked at the long lines that snaked their way across his forehead. And at his eyes that sometimes disappeared for long seconds when he blinked. His sharp boney shoulders strained against the fabric of his flannel shirt. He was still a big man, but she noticed once again how very old he had become, and how very tired.

Rheena and her little brother moved in close to get a better look at *ewe*. They stood one on either side of the drum. Zachary stretched out his small brown hand and touched the top of the drum then quickly withdrew it. He clenched his fist and kneaded his fingertips against his palm. He was certain that he had felt something. He looked at his empty hand to see what it was. Rheena looked too. There was nothing there.

The sound that had been reverberating outside lessened slightly. Finally, it disappeared into a vague memory. Silence hung in the air like a wet cloth. If they hadn't heard the thundering, then they certainly heard the silence that followed.

Papa picked up the drum and studied it. Then he carried it back to its place in the corner. When the cover was in place his voice broke the quiet.

"Ewe call to you when he ready to talk."

In the days that followed, no one mentioned the thunderstorm that never arrived. Or the uneasy feeling that accompanied it. Hoban never teased Rheena about the picture. No one mentioned ewe. And now, when Rheena or Zachary approached Papa's bedroom at the top of the stairs, they slowed down just enough to hurry by. If the bedroom door was open, they resisted the impulse to go inside. If Papa was sitting in his high back chair, as he did more and more these days, they stopped only long enough to make polite greetings before hurrying on their way. Whenever possible they stole brave glances at the mud cloth that covered the talking drum. But never a word was uttered about ewe.

3

Off to School

IF SHE HAD TO pick her worst days ever, Rheena would include this first day of school. It all started that morning at 7:30 when she boarded the elementary school bus instead of the middle school bus.

She and Zachary walked to the bus stop just beyond the stone column entrance to Clifton Avenue. They were the first to arrive. She wore her new sneakers, perfect for standing and looking nice in her pleated skirt and white blouse printed with the Adinkra Mate Masie design all over it. Papa had picked it out, and only because purple was her favorite color, and the design looked more like eyes than an African symbol, did she agree to wear it. Her socks made her feet hot and the school day was only just beginning.

Zachary wore a brand-new pair of stiff-legged jeans and a T-shirt with *"Save the Dolphins"* printed under a drawing of an ocean of dolphins. He never cared much about how he looked but Rheena knew his new shoes hurt his feet too. Mama had given him some of the medicine that would help him stay calm and focused. Still, he rocked back and forth scoring little trenches in the grass where he stood.

The two hadn't waited long before other girls and boys began to arrive at the school bus stop. They walked up, ran over or drove with their moms or dads from different streets to also wait for the yellow bus. Some of the girls she recognized. In fact, some of them she had played with during the summer. Now, however, they fell into familiar school cliques, none of which was she a member. So, Rheena stood in silence next to her brother as he rocked and while the others chattered about their summer vacation and new classroom assignments.

The high school bus came first. It had no distinguishing marks other than the mob of teenagers that crowded around. Hoban strolled up nonchalantly at the last minute and stepped onto the bus never once looking in his sister and brother's direction or at any of the other high school students who crowded noisily in front of him.

Two more yellow buses pulled up and smaller children tumbled out of cars and vans that had been parked along the road. Their moms made a show of hugging and kissing these little ones and Rheena was glad she didn't have to endure that humiliation, though the children seem to lavish in the attention. Two more buses pulled up and took the place of the first two. Rheena and Zachary joined most of the remaining children as they climbed aboard. A third bus took on the remaining children.

It was the first time Rheena had been on a yellow school bus. In Brooklyn, she walked the six blocks to P.S. 68. Here on the bus, feet and book bags cluttered the narrow center aisle of a bus. Children jostled for seats, and she wondered when they had gotten their seat assignments. She would have liked to be seated by the window but was stuck two aisle seats from her brother, the only empty spots left on the bus.

There were seat belts, but no one bothered with them, so she didn't either. The straight back seats were hard and uncomfortable; the road was extremely bumpy. The air was already cloyed by a failed attempt to mask the smell of last semester's old lunches, dirty socks and children tired from a long day. After 45 noisy minutes of driving through the neighborhood, stopping for new passengers before driving to the next bus stop, they arrived at the school. Just as quickly as they boarded, Rheena, Zachary and the rest of children were lined up and pointed in the direction of the one-story brick and glass building.

As Rheena stood in line among the unfamiliar girls and boys, she thought about P.S 68, her old school in Brooklyn. There she had left her friends and all the things that were familiar. The Brooklyn school building was four stories high. It had two sets of staircases and an elevator that went from the basement all the way to the fourth floor.

The elevator to the basement, of course, was only for the janitorial staff. But the kids who had problems walking, like Jenny Edwards who was in a wheelchair, or Bobby Thompson, who broke his leg once, and the kids who had trouble breathing or keeping up, got special permission to ride the elevator. Even then, these kids hardly ever rode the elevator, except for Jenny Edwards; she always rode the elevator.

The first floor of the Brooklyn public school had enough rooms to hold the nurse's office, the principal's office, the guidance counselor's office, the multipurpose room where they had gym and assembly, the kindergarteners and the first graders. On the second floor were the second and third graders. The third floor had the fourth and fifth graders. The fourth floor was for the sixth graders where, Rheena mused, she should be sitting with her friends, the art club, and the school newspaper. The students who had a special interest in writing and painting and drawing rode the elevator to the fourth floor. The floor she, sadly, would now never get to be on.

The line of students outside of this one-story brick and glass school building began its slow move again. It passed the lady with a forced smile and a blue plastic clipboard filled with pages of names of students, teachers and room numbers. Rheena heard the lady repeat Zachary's last name and then his first. She watched as her brother disappeared into the building. Soon would be her turn. Her mind wandered as she waited.

Here upstate, all of the kindergarteners, first graders and second graders had three different school buildings from which to choose. The older children were kept separate from the little kids by an entire building. These older kids attended the middle school and the high school.

Rheena looked at the signage over the door. With alarm she realized that this was one of the three elementary schools! Behind her, second and third graders waited as patiently as they could. Not fourth, fifth and sixth graders. She was a sixth grader! She was at the wrong school. She had gotten on the wrong bus! This was one of the three elementary schools! Not her middle school!

Across the expansive parking lot, through the stand of pine and maple trees Rheena could see the middle school. She could see her new school. Over there, the buses, at least one of which she should have been on, was just disgorging its fourth, fifth and sixth grade passengers. They weren't on any line. They moved freely and independently from the bus and into the school building. They called to and waved at their sixth-grade friends and classmates. And she was not included. This first day of school was getting off to a very bad start.

Rheena pushed her way back through the line of first and second graders. She clutched her book bag to her chest and sprinted crossed the parking lot toward the middle school building and her real classmates. Now that she was weaving her way between the parked vehicles and across the blacktop, the lot was much larger than she had realized. Rheena reached the edge of the parking area and stepped over the foot-high wire fence and onto the red cedar mulch that covered the ground. She waded through the blades of lilyturf.

Papa called this ground cover "monkey grass" and it seemed to grow everywhere. Its few remaining spikey white and lavender flowers snagged her socks and left white scratch marks where her legs were bare. Dark berries squished under the soles of her new sneakers and stained their canvas tops. Rheena pushed the low hanging spruce branches aside, before she reached a shallow two feet wide stream. She could hear the voices of her classmates and teachers growing fainter through the trees on the other side of the stream.

Rheena pulled the strap of her book bag over her head and tossed the messenger bag the short distance across the water. It landed on the grass with a thump. She leaped across the water behind the bag, landed on her hands and knees, picked up her book bag and scurried up the side of the embankment in time to see the school bus monitor enter the building and the doors close.

Rheena raced across the road designated *"bus lane only,"* and up the walkway to the Middle School door. She pulled and pushed on one door's long silver bar then the others. All of the doors were locked. She cupped both hands against her face and peered through the narrow strip of glass. The hallway was empty. Inside a bell rang.

Rheena followed the pathway around the perimeter of the building. She skirted past walls of windowpanes and doors with no handles or knobs before finally reaching the front of the building. Three-foot high letters over the entrance proclaimed it to be the Monticello Middle School. Thankfully, this door was not locked. She brushed the dirt from her clothes, secured the strap of her book bag over her shoulder, combed her fingers through her locks and entered the unfamiliar building.

With no one to tell her where to go she went to the desk under the bold sign hanging from the ceiling; INFORMATION! All Visitors Must Sign in Here! A woman wearing a flowery silk blouse, her glasses perched on the tip of her nose, glanced up from her telephone conversation. With a look of reproach, she assessed Rheena from head to toe. Rheena's sneakers were stained with drying mud and berry juice, burrs still clung to her socks. Both of her knees were scrapped. There were pine needles and leaves in her hair, and her blouse was sweaty from her dash across the parking lot, the stream and up the embankment.

"You're late!" the hall monitor scolded.

"I ..." Rheena began.

"Who's your teacher?" she continued.

"I don't..." Rheena stammered.

"I gotta go," the lady said into the mouthpiece of the telephone before punching a button on the console and cradling the receiver. "What's your name, then?" she barked as she swiveled around in her chair and snapped open the folder in front of her.

Rheena tilted her chin into the air and faced the Middle School hall monitor. *"You keep your chin up Rheena Mackey, no matter what's going on,"* her mother always told her. The woman glowered at her over the rim of her glasses. Rheena squared her shoulders.

"My name is Rheena Mackey!" she said with only a slight quiver in her voice. The woman examined her a moment longer, then turned her gaze to the folder on the desk.

"M! M! M! McCoy, McGee, Mackey!" the hall monitor slid a colorfully manicured fingernail down the list of names. "Here you are, Miss Mackey, Rheena! Room 42. Your teacher is Ms. Segala." She scribbled on a sheet of paper and pulled the page from the folder. "Are you related to Gerald Mackey?" the woman continued, her tone slightly softer.

"Yes. He's my grandfather," Rheena said. "We're living with him, now," she added.

"Your grandfather is a very nice man," the hall monitor said smiling.

"Thank you," Rheena said not quite sure if it was the appropriate response. The hall monitor handed her a yellow slip of paper.

"You're in the purple section."

Rheena shoved the hall pass into her messenger bag and walked in the direction the woman pointed. Closed doors and empty bulletin boards lined the walls on either side of her. The soles of her shoes made a squeak-squeak, squeak-squeak sound as she hastened toward her classroom number 42. She was met at the end of the hallway by another corridor that went to the left and to the right. Purple tiles patterned the walls and floor to the right. Green tiles, the walls and floor to the left. Rheena turned right. The #42 was mounted on a small metal plate beside the second classroom door. Rheena pushed open the door. Eighteen pairs of eyes looked in her direction.

"Welcome!" Ms. Segala said sarcastically as she glanced at the wall clock in the back of the room. The teacher pointed to an empty desk and chair on the opposite side of the room nearest the window. Apparently, adults did a lot of pointing in the Monticello Middle School. Self-conscious and stiff-legged, Rheena walked to her seat.

"You've missed our introduction, …" Ms. Segala glanced down at the attendance book on her desk, "Miss Mackey. But I guess we'll remember you as the late comer and no further introduction will be needed." She smiled kindly before continuing.

"Do you have a late pass?"

"Yes, ma'am."

Rheena foraged through her book bag while her new sixth grade teacher and classmates watched and waited. Somehow the yellow slip of paper had wedged itself in the bottom of the bag between her cucumber sandwich and her three-ring binder. With some effort she retrieved the wrinkled paper and extended it to Ms. Segala, who made no movement in Rheena's direction.

Chastened, Rheena stood again, knocking her bag and most of its contents on to the floor. Someone to her right snickered. Rheena handed the late pass to the teacher then squatted to pick up her belongings. Dried mud covered her socks and shoes. Bits of grass still clung to her bag. To clean them now would only draw more attention to her appearance. So, she sat back down, crossed her ankles, and tucked her feet under her chair.

"Jeffrey," said Ms. Segala after a few seconds of silence. "Please give Rhianna an ELA text and workbook."

"It's Rheena." Rheena corrected.

"There will be no shouting out in class. Raise your hand if you have something to say," said the teacher.

A too-tall 10-year-old, jug-eared boy with red hair, cut short for a crisp back-to-school look, crossed the room to the supply closet and brought Rheena a hard cover and a soft cover book. He dropped them on her desk with a curt:

"Here!" To which she muttered:

"Thanks!"

"Okay, let's get back to work," continued Ms. Segala from her seat at her desk. "Turn to page 7. You should have all read chapters 1 and 2 over the summer break. So, let's review."

Rheena's first day of school got only slightly better. She was able to follow the other students to math class and then to the far side of the building to the cafeteria for lunch. She recognized some of the boys and girls from the neighborhood. Several of them had come to the big ice cream party Papa had in his yard.

Papa Gerald Mackey had invited all of the kids in the area to celebrate the end of summer vacation. One last day of fun before getting back to the business of learning, he called it.

"Dis way, you meet all da new school mates, maybe even make a friend or two," he suggested as they drove around the neighborhood handing out colorful index cards penciled with YOU ARE INVITED and drawings of balloon and drums, flowers and yellow, brown and pink circles atop cone-shaped triangles. There was homemade ice cream and tons of fried fish at the backyard party. There were musicians and face painters, all hosted by Papa so that the neighborhood kids could get to know each other.

For all the good it did. No one in the lunchroom spoke with her or offered to sit next to her. No more ice cream parties for this crowd, Rheena vowed.

Bells rang throughout the building. Every 40 minutes the sound signaled the change of a period. For a few minutes after the bell the hallway was crowded and noisy with students changing classes. The bell rang a few minutes later signaling the start of the next period. Then the hallway was quiet. Rheena followed the students in her homeroom as they paraded through the hall. Sometimes she and the others went to a different room, sat for forty minutes, and then went back to homeroom #42. Most of the time they put away one set of books and took out a new set. After one chaotic march through the hallway, she followed the others into a classroom to discover during *the attendance,* she was in the wrong place.

"Check *your schedule!*" the teacher in the front of the room curtly admonished as she gathered her things and hurried out. Fortunately, she located the correct room, found an empty seat to fill before *the attendance* was taken and the second bell sounded.

She hoped that Zachary and Hoban were having a better first day than she was.

Across town, Hoban's first day of school was only slightly better than his little sister's. Despite his best effort, he had not been able to adjust to life outside of Brooklyn. First of all, the comfortable grid layout of the streets that was downstate was painfully lacking upstate. Also missing from these streets were the continuous sound of rubber tires rolling on asphalt, blaring car horns, the wail of sirens, angry outburst and joyful laughter. There was no corner anything that served as a destination. No place to go except somebody's house. No place to hang out, except in the woods. Nothing to do, except play video games.

The teens his age idled about, seemingly without purpose. He quickly became the cool kid from the city. They all looked to him for something to do. However, Hoban knew he was not cool, and he was nobody's leader. If he wanted to sneak and smoke a cigarette or a joint, which he did not; or hide and drink beer, also not on his must-do list, he preferred to do it by himself. He just wanted to be left alone.

The karate school that he'd once enjoyed had lost its appeal. That was most likely because at 17, he was much older than the other students. So, for most of the summer he went there only to solo on the makiwara, or to practice his katas and foot work. He never even bothered to Gi up.

Some days he would be at the dojo for hours, as waves of little kids came and went, kia'd and spared. He punched and kicked, pretending to be Bruce Lee, or Ali who both rightfully proclaimed that they were the greatest. Not Hoban Cruz, the nobody with nothing, who no one listened to. When he completed his dojo workouts, sweaty and exhausted, imaginary opponents and invisible foes lay crumpled at his feet, victims of his powerful spinning roundhouse kick. He would jog home and fall asleep on the living room sofa, wishing he were anywhere but here.

Now, on the first day of his senior year, he would have to start life all over again. He had made up his mind earlier, as he lay on his back on the sofa where he slept most nights, waiting for the rest of the house to wake up, that he was not even going to bother with school. Maybe not forever, but certainly for today. He would walk to town and catch the first Shortline bus to Westchester.

He had his dad's work schedule memorized. He would ride to Tarrytown, walk to his dad's apartment where they would talk about guy stuff. Things he could not talk to his mother about. They would order lunch: pizza, pulled pork sandwiches, Chinese, empanadas, anything they wanted, and eat together on the sofa, Latin music pulsing in the background. After their third or fourth slice or egg roll, or empanada, Mama drew the dietary line with processed foods, his dad would tell him how lucky he was to be living with his mother instead of with him. Hoban would argue with his dad that he was wrong.

"Pops, look around this place. You got it made!"

His dad's apartment was neat, sparsely furnished, but neat. Nothing extra to clutter up his life. That was a rule: *Take nothing you don't need.* His dad had a rule for just about every situation.

At some point during the visit, his dad would tell him to *man-up!* He'd remind his son of the rules for safe living. He'd tell him how much his mother needed him!

"*You know how mom can be!*" Hoban would lament.

"*Oh, don't I!*" his dad would say, and they would laugh.

Next, his dad would tell him: "*it's getting late, m'hijo*" and he would give him a few dollars, and put him on the bus back home.

The two had performed this ritual, or variations of the ritual countless times. Hoban needed the connection. He was glad for the connection. And deep down he was always glad that his dad put him on the bus and sent him back home.

He played this scenario over in his mind as he walked down Clifton Avenue. Then he saw his little sister and brother waiting by the school bus sign. Rheena, the little stinker, he could tell, was nervous. She was standing, her knees hyperextended, locked back, her hands gripping the strap of her messenger-style book bag. She was chewing on the inside of her lower lip. How many times had he instructed her about standing like that?

"*You make yourself weak and vulnerable!*" he would caution. "*Bend your knees a little bit! Like this.*" Then he would bounce lightly on the balls of his feet, his knees slightly bent, his dark curly hair bouncing on his head. And Rheena would snicker at him and run off.

"She's such a little pain in the butt!" he muttered as he watched her waiting for the school bus.

Zachary, he saw, had his hands shoved into his pants pockets. He rocked, head down, from side to side all the while staring at his feet as they dug tiny ruts into the dirt. He was such a bundle of energy and every moment with him was an adventure. Hoban knew that it was best that they not see him skipping out on the school bus. They ought not know that he was ditching school. So, he joined the other high school students and boarded the bus. He decided he would take off from school after homeroom.

His first period after homeroom was math. Instead of heading down the hall, as his class schedule directed, when the first bell rang, Hoban followed the noisy flow of foot traffic downstairs.

Near the front door, the school security officer chatted playfully with several of the other high school students. Despite the man's relaxed stance and his overly familiar attitude, Hoban knew he wouldn't be leaving the building through that door. Hoban prepared to push his shoulder against the door nearest him when he heard a voice.

"Hey! Brooklyn!" came the whisper. "This way!"

He turned to see a boy with a backward facing baseball cap leaning into a door farther down the hall. Hoban chanced a glance in the direction of the security guard then turned to watch as the teen disappeared through the door. He followed.

The door opened onto a stairwell where the teen in the backward baseball cap waited with three others. Hoban descended the five stairs in two steps and followed the quartet outside. Green dumpsters and unoccupied cars and pick-up trucks lined the wall of the building. The truants darted between parked vehicles and walked stealthily into the wooded area that flanked the back of the building. After several hundred feet of climbing over rocks that threatened to trip them and pulling through fallen tree limbs, they emerged into a backyard. They trotted through the yard, vaulted the chain-link fence, and hurried down the driveway. A large dog barked from inside the house. The five teens power walked on the uneven sidewalk until the dog stopped. They stopped.

"Yo! That was crazy, man!" backward baseball cap kid exclaimed.

They broke into riotous laughter relieving the tension that gripped them for the past 10 minutes.

"Kev, I didn't think you was comin'!" said the boy with braces in his mouth to the teen with the backwards cap.

"What kept ya?"

It was a girl's voice. Hoban turned for the first time to the fourth member of the pack. Her shoulder length blonde hair was pulled back behind her ears; however, he should have noticed she was female, despite the baggy jeans, how her T-shirt clung to her body. *Rule #10*, Hoban reminded himself: *Pay attention!*

"Healy actually checked attendance. Can you believe it? The first day and he wants to do a meet and greet," said Kev.

They chuckled some more and started walking in the direction of what Hoban hoped was Broadway. He was helplessly lost and would have to depend on this motley mob for a while longer.

"I'm Morris," said the boy with the braces. "This here is Kev, that's Joey and Maven," he said indicating with a nod of his head the boy and girl who walked behind them.

"So, Brooklyn. You got a name?" asked Kev.

"Brooklyn's fine," said Hoban.

"Sweet!" said Morris.

"I gotta get me a handle," Joey added after a pause.

"My name is my handle," Maven said sarcastically. "That's all I need!" she added with pride. "See that house right there?" she said with a nod of her head in the direction of the house they were passing. "I babysit for the two kids there. You can't tell for looking at their place; but they are loaded!" she said. "I mean lo-o-o-oaded! He works on Wall Street or something," she added for emphasis. "And the lady in there," she indicated another house as they passed a yard filled with flowers and garden gnomes, "she could be on that show where they film crazy people who collect too much stuff."

"Hoarders?" said Joey.

"Yeah, Hoarders," said Maven.

For the next 10 minutes Maven identified points of interest, if only to her, to the group that shadowed Hoban through the residential streets. After another five minutes of walking, Hoban could hear the sound of Broadway traffic. He knew now where he was. The bus station was behind the Government Center. Hoban picked up his pace. There was no need to continue to hang back with these four. He broke into a trot, quickly closing the distance between him and the bus station. The little mob followed him as he turned onto York Avenue headed for Pelton. Maven saw the car first.

"Guys!" she said interrupting her own litany of people and events.

Maven slowed her run to a fast walk. Their eyes followed hers to the police car idling at the end of the street. Hoban noted the driver's downward gaze in the car's side-view mirror. The officer had not noticed them. They were behind him. Kev reversed his jog. Morris and Joey fast walked across the street and up the driveway between two houses Maven had moments earlier identified as vacant, leaving Kev, Maven and their new pal Brooklyn in plain sight. The movement of Hoban's unsolicited posse must have alerted the police officer because he looked up, first into his rearview mirror and then into the side view mirror. He saw them.

Kev and Maven ran. The deputy made an effortless U-turn and pulled the squad car to a swift stop alongside Hoban blocking his retreat. He got out of the patrol car retrieved his cap and placed it deliberately on his head. The effect was complete.

Hoban slowly raised his arms out to his sides. He knew the drill. Cops, he knew, were all the same. Once they put on their uniform, they became a gang of their own: not Black, not white, not Hispanic, not even female. Just cops. They had the uniform, and they had the gun. If it were just a dude strapping a gun, Hoban was certain he would know how to handle himself. A dude strapping and wearing a uniform. That was a different animal. The rules were different.

The police officer adjusted his belt and sauntered slowly to where Hoban stood motionless. Hoban could see that the man was taking his measure, just as Hoban was taking his. He was dominant to the right. His baton hung awkwardly at his left hip. He was nervous. Never a good sign, Hoban noted. Nervous men with guns, who also wore uniforms, often did stupid things. *Rule 27a: Nervous people do stupid things. #27b: nervous people who have guns and wear uniforms, … well you never can tell.*

"Early dismissal?" the deputy asked.

Right hand at the ready, the deputy ran deft fingers of his left hand along Hoban's chest, his back and up and down the inside and outside of both of his legs. The officer was so vulnerable. He was taking so much for granted. He had a gun, and he wore a uniform.

"Sort of," answered Hoban tolerating the frisk.

"Where'd your friends go?" he asked.

"They're not my friends." Hoban said.

"Obviously." He held his fingertips against Hoban's chest as he reached with his other hand for the handcuffs hooked at his waist. Hoban could have easily blocked the gesture by bringing his own hands up, crossing them at the wrist, pushing the man's hand to the side. Fast enough and with enough force the move would have thrown the cop off balance giving Hoban time to bolt across the hood of the patrol car and between the two vacant houses. He decided against it. *Rule # 2: Don't start a fight you can't finish.*

Instead, in a matter of seconds, the cuffs were on Hoban's wrist and his hands secured behind his back. The policeman directed Hoban over to the patrol car.

"Get in!" he said as he opened the back door of his car. With one hand on top of Hoban's mop of long black hair, he guided Hoban into the backseat. After a few inaudible words spoken into the microphone to the dispatcher they drove in silence through town, past the bus station where the bus to Westchester was pulling out, and to the police station.

The policeman parked the patrol car at the curb and escorted his capture inside, transferred his custody over to the desk sergeant with a few whispered words, removed Hoban's restraints and left.

Hoban stood nervously against the wall. He refused to sit on the dirty wooden bench beside him. *Rule #22: Don't sit if you can stand.*

"How come I don't know you?" the desk sergeant asked Hoban after several tense minutes. He pushed his thumb along his chin as if he expected to find his answer hidden somewhere deep in the folds of flesh.

"I can't answer that for you, sir." Hoban responded respectfully.

"What's your name?" he asked as he still toyed with his chin.

"Hoban Cruz." Hoban answered.

"Where you live, Hoban Cruz?" As he leaned in to write, the seams at the shoulder of the man's shirt strained against his considerable size.

Hoban almost said Brooklyn, and then remembered as of two months ago, he no longer had a home there. He thought of giving his father's address in Tarrytown. That could explain why he was on the street during what ought to be school hours. He would say that he was headed to the bus terminal so that he could go home. Either answer would suffice; either answer would also come dangerously close to violating *Rule #12: Be discreet.*

"Monticello," he answered. The man grunted a sigh and scribbled something with the pen he held in his free hand.

"You wanna call somebody?" he asked without looking up from his scrawling.

The big man rolled his chair from the desk so that he could retrieve a telephone from the top draw of the table behind him. He slammed the cellular phone onto his desk in Hoban's reach.

Hoban wasn't sure whom to call. His dad would still be at work. His mother was also not likely to answer a call. He flipped the phone open, paused a second, then punched in the phone number of the house on Clifton Street. He listened to the phone ringing at the other end. He didn't know what Papa did during the day but did know that unless Rheena or Mama answered a call, the phone could ring eight, even 10 times before Papa answered. On the ninth ring Hoban prepared to snap the phone closed when the line opened.

"Hello," he heard Papa's voice.

"Papa, it's me, Hoban," he said humbly.

There was a long silence. Hoban could hear Papa's breathing on the other end of the line.

"You okay, son?" Papa finally asked.

"I'm okay. I'm at ..."

"I can see where you at!" Papa interrupted him. Hoban recalled the display of name and numbers that appeared in the corner of the television screen and on the small display of the landline. It identified who was calling. He imagined Papa's face, brow furrowing into deep ridges, his lips pursed and turned down at the corners as he stared at the display. It was a mobile phone, of course he could *see where he was at*, it was displayed on the caller I.D.

"Gimme a few minutes," Papa added after a long pause.

Hoban snapped the device shut and handed it back to the desk sergeant.

"Who'd you call?" the desk sergeant asked. By law he had no right to know whom Hoban had called and no legitimate reason to ask him. Furthermore, he had not read him his Miranda Rights so technically he was not under arrest. Despite the young boy's calm demeanor, the desk sergeant could tell that the boy was nervous and inexperienced in situations like this one.

"My... I called my...," Hoban hesitated. Papa was not his grandfather. He was the father of Zachary and Rheena's father, not his. He was the father of the man who married their mother years after she and his own father broke up. He was the old man whose house he now lived in. Even though Hoban had visited Monticello several times in the last eight years the familial connection was not there for him. He was not related to Gerald Mackey; he was Cruz. He had no connection with this man's Africa, with his South, nor with his crazy ways. There was a disconnect between them. But now he had only Papa to reach out to. And without wavering, the old Black man was coming to him.

"I called my grandfather," he said at last.

The sergeant nodded and directed Hoban to sit on the well-worn wooden bench on the far side of the small room where he reluctantly say down.

As promised, it was only a few minutes that Hoban sat alone on the filthy wooden bench. Before too long the door that led to the street opened and Papa strode through. It was late summer and still warm, yet Papa wore a three-piece suit and a tie. Though the charcoal grey jacket hung loosely over his shoulder and the trouser legs bagged more than was fashionable, with his height he made a formidable entrance. The desk sergeant looked up lazily, then stood. It was a stand that stopped just short of *at attention*; he extended his hand.

"Mr. Mackey," he said with a bit of pomp and a lot of respect.

In two more steps Papa was at the desk and courteously shook the sergeant's proffered hand.

"You have my grandson here!" Papa stated rather than asked.

For an instance, a flicker of confusion, mingled with chagrin crossed the sergeant's face. He had forgotten about the boy sitting in silence on the filthy wooded bench against the wall. He looked over to where Hoban sat as his index finger joined his thumb this time at his chin. Papa followed his gaze, then turned and strode to Hoban.

Hoban understood why the desk sergeant leapt to his feet in Papa's presence. He had only seen the old man in casual dress, his shoulder and collarbones sharp under his T-shirt; in slacks with his belt cinched tight at the waist, in pajamas beneath a worn seersucker bathrobe and in slippers, or barefooted walking with an odd gait because of one leg and several toes that were missing. Now Papa stood regal and tall like one of the statues in his bedroom.

Hoban leapt to his feet as the grandfather approached him. Papa grabbed Hoban's arms with both his hands and swayed him back so that he could study Hoban's face. Hoban was nearly six feet tall; however, held in Papa's grip and under his gaze he felt small compared to the old man. Satisfied that Hoban had not been harmed in any visible way he released him and patted him gently on the side of his face.

"Let us go!" was all the old man said as they moved toward the door.

"Ah, Mr. Mackey, sir," the voice came from behind them. Papa turned but continued to guide Hoban through the door.

"We haven't arrested ...." The sergeant searched through his scribbles for Hoban's name. Not finding it he continued, "… your grandson. But we did start paperwork on him. We can't just let you take him."

Papa appeared to stretch up even taller. He stepped back to the desk even as he nudged Hoban farther out the door.

"Normally, he'd have to wait until an officer returned to take him over to the court," man continued. "He's truant. School is in session and, as you are aware, we have not solved those break-ins we've been having in the area over the past few weeks."

"My chile's no teef!" Papa firmly declared through clenched teeth.

"Of course not! Of course, I'm sure he's not; however, he was picked up with some other kids," Papa interrupted him with a quizzical look around the empty space.

"The others ran off," he amended "Your grandson didn't resist. That's to his credit," he added.

"And?" Papa asked matter-of-factly.

"There's a car out looking for the other kids now." Papa waited. "This process," the man spread his arms to include the room, his desk and the filthy wooden bench, "usually takes a while, sometimes days. But" the officer explained, "I'm going to fax these papers over to the court right now. You can head over there with young Mr. Cruz, right now, if you want." He apparently had located Hoban's name during his rambling. "With school back in session, most of the kids" he said taking care not to look in Hoban's direction, "are in class, so the court shouldn't be too crowded. I'll just need you to sign here."

Papa signed his name. "And here and here." The desk sergeant pointed to various spots on the document. He separated a leaf from the others and handed it to Gerald Mackey.

"Tank you," Papa said curtly and joined Hoban outside.

The two walked to Papa's car in silence and drove the half a block, parked and entered the courthouse without a word.

The sergeant had been wrong. It was not even 10 in the morning and the courtroom was packed with plaintiffs and defendants. Hoban and Papa tolerated the wand at the simple security checkpoint, retrieved their wallets, Hoban's cellphone, and Papa's keys from the plastic container on the table and sat down in the back of the courtroom.

It was nearly noon when a man wearing a custom-tailored charcoal gray suit came to sit down beside Hoban. He positioned his body in such a way that both Hoban and Papa were forced to turn in their place to face him.

"I'm Joseph Werner," he said without fanfare. "I work for the Public Defender's Office; however, I have a private practice as well. My personal commitment to the community is to take on a few *pro bono* cases throughout the year."

Werner looked at Gerald Mackey as he continued speaking in a quiet but articulate tone.

"Mr. Mackey, I am familiar with your work in the community. And I applaud your efforts. I understand that you have taken on the responsibility of your late son's children and their mother and I see no reason why you should bear that burden alone."

"Dey no burden," Papa responded.

"Of course not. A poor choice of words on my part. I understand how you can feel that way." He paused. The two waited.

"In addition to my practice, I have a private MMA Center that I operate out of the basement in my home." Werner shifted his gaze to Hoban. "I understand that you have an interest?" he asked.

Hoban gave a quick nod of his head. Mixed Martial Arts! Of course, I have an interest, he wanted to shout.

"A nod is not an answer," Werner chided.

"Yes, sir! I do!" Hoban corrected. He did his best to keep the excitement out of his voice. *Rule #23: Play it cool!*

"Well, then. If that be the case," he looked back to Papa. "I'd like to extend an invitation to your grandson to join our center."

"Dat be up to da boy," said Papa.

Werner's clear blue eyes turned back to Hoban. They all knew that this could be the best thing to happen in his young life.

"As I mentioned, the center is private. We have a select membership, different ages, different backgrounds. We all love the art. We all love the discipline."

He handed Hoban his business card. The scales of justice were evident in the corner. The name Joseph L. Werner preceded several elaborate black calligraphic letters.

"We have a very strict code of conduct that all of our members, me included, must adhere to," he added.

"Thank you. I'd like that very much." Hoban accepted the card.

Over at the elementary school, Zachary sat fidgeting at his new desk. He was hungry. His teacher, he had forgotten her name already, had instructed him and his classmates to store their belonging in the assigned wooden cubbies that lined the wall in the back of the room. That's where his lunch was and that's where his snack was.

She hadn't told them to empty their pockets, which was where he had a store of raisins, pieces of cashew nuts and peanuts, cookie crumbs, bits of a granola bar and the other half of the little orange pill he had swallowed with his orange juice at breakfast time earlier. Now he slipped his hand into his pants pocket where he selected, at random, a goodie which he secreted into his mouth.

He couldn't chance a look at his lap, nor could he look at the content of his hand without drawing attention to his snacking. Each nibble was a tasty surprise. Therefore, Zachary never knew what he would be eating until that first crunch of his teeth. Then the juices in his mouth would mix with the juices from, what? A raisin? No. That was a Goji berry.

Cookie crumbs were soft and moistened with his saliva faster than the bits of granola. Peanuts, he quickly discovered, posed a problem. It was their smell. His first crunch into a peanut and the entire class, including the teacher looked up and sniffed the air. He frowned and sniffed the air too, looking inquisitively around the room like everyone else.

"Miss Peterson, I smell peanut butter and jelly," the little girl at the desk behind his called out. Miss Peterson, that was her name, Zachary now recalled.

"We'll have lunch in a few minutes," said Miss Peterson.

Zachary swallowed the un-chewed peanut pieces whole. That was close. He would have to be more careful. A little pile of nuts soon grew in size in the left corner of his desk. Some, regrettably, were cashews but he couldn't take the chance. He would separate and eat them when it was safe.

Lunchtime was longer than *in just a few minutes*, as Miss Peterson had promised.

So, he played the guessing game with his mouth most of the morning as he copied the sentences from the Smartboard into his new composition notebook. No one sat to Zachary's left, where his stash of goodies accumulated inside his desk. And he wrote just as well with his right hand as he did with his left hand.

Finally, the school day was over. Rheena hopped off school bus #135 at the stone pillar and headed home. Zachary was already chasing around the backyard when she arrived. Hoban and Papa sat chatting quietly at the dining room table.

Apart from riding the wrong bus, nearly being arrested, and smelling up the classroom with the odor of peanuts, it had not gone too badly. Tomorrow they would do it all over again, but different.

4

He's Gone on Ahead

RHEENA CAME downstairs to find her mother sitting alone at the dining room table. She was nursing her usual morning cup of coffee, her hands grasping the clear mug of steamy liquid as if it would escape should she lessen her grip in the slightest. This morning was different. Papa was not sitting across from her with his glass of tea. He was not sitting there planning the day with her. Shirley sat alone staring into the cup of dark liquid.

"Morning, Mama." Rheena chirped.

Her mother continued to stare as if her daughter had not spoken. Rheena watched cautiously for a second. There was always something that her mother had to weather, and this appeared to be yet another

"S'matter, mama?" Rheena asked as she sidled over to where her mother sat and gently rubbed her hand across her mother's back, imitating the gesture her mother had done to her countless times.

"Papa's gone," Shirley whispered.

She gazed up at Rheena, her tear-stained pink eyes lingered for an instant, then dropped back down toward her coffee cup. Rheena had seen that look on her mother's face only once before. Her heart lurched in her chest as she glanced first at Papa's empty dining room chair, then up toward his bedroom at the top of the stairs. She shook her head her as she eased herself down to sit onto her mother's lap.

"Papa's not gone. He's still upstairs in his room sleep."

"No Rheena, He's left us." Shirley repeated.

Rheena pursed her lips and shook her head harder this time.

"Uh-huh," she insisted. "I saw him in his bed when I came down. You prob'bly missed him 'cause he was laying on his side looking out the window. He does that when he gets his second sleep. I do that too. I lay on my side and stare out the window. Then I get my second sleep," she explained.

Rheena was resolute, recalling the second sleep that comes after waking just before daybreak, yet not committing fully to the new day. The fullness of one's bladder usually determined how deep that second sleep would be. Rheena enjoyed second sleeps. They were so refreshing and gave her some of her best dreams; but not when they happened on a school day. School day second sleeps she dreaded, because it could take her until lunch time to recover.

Hoban sauntered downstairs and into the kitchen.

"Morning," he said in his gravelly morning voice.

He grabbed the tea kettle, shook it, then filled it to the brim with tap water before placing it on the stove and lighting a flame under it.

"I heard him laughing and talking." Rheena continued. "He was talking to his friends. And to himself too, I guess."

They all knew, from time to time, Papa had visitors come in from the neighborhood. They would stop by, often unannounced to chat about the happening things in the community, about things of the past, about plans for the future, *dis'n dat*, as Papa'd put it. There would often be visits that went on late into the night; long after the rest of the house had gone to sleep; there'd be voices prattling, and plates clattering. Last night must have been one of those visitation nights because Rheena had heard their grandfather chatting and laughing and crooning in that sing-song voice of his.

But Papa never entertained in his bedroom, though. Rather, he'd slowly climb up the stairs to retrieve a box filled to near bursting with photos, or buttons and odd trinkets, or a folder swollen with news clippings or sheets of pages crinkled at the edges. These he'd bring downstairs to spread out onto the dining room table. His guest would *humph! ooh!* and *aah!* Sometimes an *amen!* was uttered, or an outburst of laughter would fill the space. The next morning, however, you would never know anyone had even been over. The house would, once again, be quiet and spotlessly clean. No dishes in the sink, no boxes or folders left out. Occasionally, an errant slip of paper with a phone number jotted on it might be found on the coffee table.

"He was talking about a boat. He said: *'Somebody hep me row my boat.'*" Rheena told them imitating Papa's voice

"*Help me row my boat*? Hoban repeated mockingly, as he rummaged through the kitchen cabinet for his mug and then into the tea tin for his favorite teabag.

"I heard him say it! *'Who's gonna hep me row my boat?'* is what he said," Rheena insisted.

"Papa ain't got no boat, *tontita*!" Hoban added for good measure.

"I suppose he knew." A sob stuttered in Shirley's throat.

Hoban turned toward his mother for the first time since coming into the kitchen.

"Knew what?" Concern edged into Hoban's voice. "What's the matter, Ma?" he asked her.

"Papa's gone," she said.

"No, Mama. I told you he's in his room," Rheena said.

Hoban's gaze darted from his mother to sister then toward the stairs.

"You mean, … like *gone* gone?" he asked staring into the inner regions of their home.

She nodded and fought to hold back her crying.

"Like *dead* and gone?" Hoban tactlessly clarified.

"Yes. During the night," she began again.

"But…," Rheena started to speak.

"Papa has gone on ahead," Shirley simply said.

In two steps Hoban bridged the gap between his mother and his little sister. He moved from the kitchen and across the room. His outstretched arms reaching to embrace the two. With one hand Hoban cradled his mother's head against his chest; with the other he scrunched a fist full of his little sister's hair where they sat. The pleasantly familiar scent of coconut oil wafted into his nostrils. He pulled them gently into his embrace. Together they joined hearts, swaying in their mutual grief. In those same two steps Hoban took to reach them, with that single gesture of compassion, his life was irrevocably changed.

Hoban did not feel saddened at this loss. Papa was not his grandfather, not his kin. Truth be told, despite all the love and affection shown to him by the old Black man, Hoban never genuinely felt it in his heart to reciprocate. Gerald Mackey was Rheena and Zachary's grandfather, not his. Yes, he was grateful for a roof over his head. He was grateful that the old man's influence kept him out of court, possibly out of jail even. He did his best to show that appreciation. He was always respectful. He was always helpful. He was always grateful. *Rule #8: Don't be ungrateful.* But he knew *Rule #12* told him to *Be authentic: Don't be a phony.* He could not feel what he didn't feel.

Yet, as he held his mother and his sister, he felt something. That something overwhelmed him. It was fear. And that fear mingled with Shirley's grief and Rheena's uncertainty. He was afraid that, as the old Black man had gone on, had died during the night, had died without fanfare, he, Hoban Cruz, had to step in as the man in the house. *Step up or step back*! That was a numberless rule. Tears flowed unbidden from his eyes.

Zachary sauntered downstairs and saw his family. Without asking what, without knowing why, he too began to cry. He fell into his mother's arm as Hoban included the little boy in his embrace. After those moments together for the first time in this way, Hoban was never the same. He was transformed from man child to manhood. From deep within, he was now giving, no longer merely taking.

The sudden shrill whistle of the tea kettle startled Hoban from his reverie. He left his mother's side to turn off the flame and to dial 911. Within moments, the emergency vehicle's flashing lights had drawn a crowd outside Gerald Mackey's Clifton Avenue home to watch the cortege of medics roll their beloved paterfamilias out of the house, down the driveway and into the coroner's van.

The days that followed Papa Gerald Mackey's death were equally as mournful as they were celebratory. Rheena and Zachary watched in awe from their perch on the staircase as a multiplicity of plain folk and dignitaries paraded in and out of their Clifton Avenue home. From noon to midnight, they came and went. These people laughed and they cried, several pattering in the South Sea Island patois. They were young. They were old. They wore suits and ties, jeans and plaid shirts, dresses long and short. They wore big hats, no hats, turbans, dukus and geles. Black clothes, white clothes, African print, Kente cloth, mud cloth and denim. Some wore uniforms with sidearms, others with just a colorful array of shields, badges and bars pinned above their left breast pocket and lapels.

There was no end to the variety of sweet and spicy music and food that Rheena and Zachary heard and ate. One day, the celebration spilled out onto the sidewalk, with Rheena and Zachary and several other children running in play, while people danced to the loud Motown sound blaring from car speakers. Another day there was silence and prayers.

Men and women who had been pictures on the wall, on the mantel or displayed in frames on the sideboard, patted Rheena on her cheek, or cupped her chin while they muttered words she no longer listened to. Most days, Mama, attired always in a long colorful house dress, moved through the crowd, or she sat quietly in the dining room next to Papa's chair, which had been draped in a plush blue velvet cloth. The other days she stayed in her bedroom and slept. Hoban stayed away from it all.

Finally, by the end of the week, a long line of cars, led by the black car with the casket and body of Gerald Mackey, rolled quietly through the village, onto the highway and out of town. Rheena and Zachary and their mother Shirley remained behind in the big house that had welcomed them, that had winked slyly at them, that sheltered them. Papa had gone on ahead.

5

Back in Time

ZACHARY MACKEY pulled his feet into the safety of his bedclothes then elbowed the cover over his head, leaving a spider's width for breathing. From outside the shelter of his bed there was a bright flash. Dark followed the flash. He peered into the unpredictable darkness and counted:

"One! Two! Three!"

Clash! Rumble! Rumble! Thunder roared immediately after the lightning brightened the sky. The heavy rain pummeled a frightful rhythm on the rooftop. Blue-white flashes lit the pre-dawn sky. The storm was moving quickly now. Flash! Rumble! Rumble! Zachary lolled back in the bed as the April thunderstorm rattled through the Catskills.

He waited for the familiar Saturday morning smells of hot oatmeal with cinnamon, butter and honey to waft its way upstairs and into his bedroom. It never came. That meant Mama had gone to work early and Rheena was "in charge" until either Hoban came home, or their mother returned from work. Flash!

"One! Two! Thr...!"

Clash! Flash! Flash! BOOM! Rumble! Rumble! The house shook. On a day like today Zachary would have to plan very carefully if he was to avoid trouble from his older brother or sister.

The sound of the steady pounding of rain on the roof grew in anger. Zachary closed his eyes and monitored the lightning flashes through his lids. Flash! Rumble! Rumble! He soon drifted back to sleep.

In the bedroom next door, Rheena watched the blue gray dawn force its way through the rain. She felt, rather than heard, her mother open the bedroom door. Shirley tiptoed in before softly calling her daughter's name. Rheena measured her breathing, keeping it slow and dreamlike. She pretended to be asleep. The trick she had mastered by the time she was Zachary's age almost always guaranteed her at least an extra 15 minutes in bed.

"Rheena?" Shirley Mackey whispered, her voice gentle, as always soothing.

The lilt in her voice signaled she was just checking to see if her daughter was awake or asleep. Rheena took a deep breath and let it out like a measured sigh. It made her sound as if she were just on the edge of wakefulness where her mother would let her linger. Papa called it the edges of sleep, a magical time, and said to never call anyone from their sleep too abruptly.

"I'm gonna leave a little early, sweetheart," she said.

"Uh huh." Rheena sighed.

"It's really coming down hard out there," Shirley muttered to herself concern in her voice.

She peered out the window at the sheets of water falling from the sky. Flashes of light lit the morning sky. The exploding sound of thunder roiled overhead. Shirley lowered the window shade.

"You and Zach stay close. Okay?" she said.

"Uh huh."

Shirley kissed her daughter's forehead and pulled the covers snug up around her shoulders.

"Go back to sleep," she whispered. Rheena did.

Lightning flashed blue white. The ensuing thunder competed with the electronic anthem of the seven animated robots as they lined up, side by side across the television screen. Their brightly colored alien uniforms identifying them and their powers.

Zachary was up first. It was early and Rheena was still in bed. By default, he had earned the honor command of the channel blaster. Until she came downstairs and wrestled the remote from him, he could maintain control of Saturday morning entertainment.

The penciled message on a heart-shaped pink notepaper stuck on the refrigerator door was clear:

"*I have a nine o'clock,*" it read, "*get some cold cereal. Don't turn on the stove!!!* There were three exclamation points. "*Hoban, fix your brother and sister something hot for breakfast. I'll be back by one. Love, Mom*"

A second piece of heart shaped paper, this one yellow, was stuck next to the first. It read: "*Nobody in! Nobody out!*"

Their mother kept the same page with its smiley face drawing and reused it whenever she had to be away and wanted to maintain long distance control of the house. Not that it ever made much of a difference as to whether they went into the yard. At least, however, they knew not to stray too far from the house. Hoban wasn't home.

It was the sound of the television blaring that next woke Rheena. She opened her eyes to little slits so that the early morning light could nudge its way into her consciousness. She could see the flowers she and her mother had planted in egg cartons. Resting on the outer edge on the windowsill, tiny shoots were just peeking their heads out of the soil. The rain beat down on them hard.

Zachary was pouring his third bowl of Crunchy Pops and milk by the time Rheena idled lazily downstairs. Dreary weather made Rheena dreamy and rainy weather subdued her to a place that as little brother, Zachary, could manage.

"Anymore left?" Rheena yawned. Her lion mane of tangled braids bounced against her shoulders. Tweety Bird smiled, one eyebrow raised mischievously, from the front of her nightshirt. Rheena slid into her place at the table. She scratched her backside unceremoniously.

"That is absolutely disgusting at the table, Rheena."

"I'm itching at the table, Zach!" she said turning the one syllable of his name into two distinct sounds.

Rheena spilled the last of the Crunchy Pops into her bowl, shook the empty milk carton and then began spooning the dry cereal into her mouth.

"Where's Mama?" She snaked out her tongue and caught one of the dry yellow kernels that somehow managed to hang onto her top lip despite her vigorous chewing.

"She had braids to do," Zachary informed her.

"Where's Hoban?" Rheena strained her neck to read the smiley face posted on the refrigerator door behind her chair.

"Don't know!"

"Why'd she tell him to fix us something to eat if he ain't even here?"

"Don't know!" Zachary answered again.

"I'm gonna make me some eggs," Rheena announced. "Want some?"

"Mama said: Don't turn on the stove!" He poked his index finger on each word of the note for emphasis as Rheena made a slapdash circle of the kitchen to collect the ingredients for scrambled eggs. She spilled cooking oil from the mayonnaise jar on the stove into a frying pan, turned on the flame under the pan, then cracked open three eggs and let them drop side by side into the oil. Zachary peeled slices of cheese from their plastic cover and laid them on top of the eggs that were just beginning to change form in the heating oil.

Outside the storm strobed and vibrated the village. Ribbons of electricity fluttered in the air and disappeared. Sheets of spring rain cascaded down the street and ponded on the lawns and driveways, spilling into basements through windows, cracks and stairs.

The electronic cartoon noises that blared from the television in the living room pinged out for an instant then resumed. The kitchen lights flickered for several seconds. The two children exchanged alarmed glances before the television went silent and the light was sucked up by darkness.

Rheena pulled her body onto the kitchen counter to peer out the window over the sink. She could barely make out the outline of Denny Harrison's house across the yard. It was too dark out. Of course, it was just seven in the morning. Not many people would be up this early on Saturday. It was impossible to tell if it was the storm or late sleepers.

During their first Monticello winter, Papa and Shirley had prepared Rheena, Hoban and Zachary for power outages. Nevertheless, they never quite grew accustomed to being suddenly plunged into complete darkness. If it was just the a bad fuse, they knew what to do. If it were the whole village, they would have to wait it out until power was restored.

Rheena retrieved the flashlight from behind the breadbox, clicked it on and made her way to the hall stairs. Behind her, Zachary followed, his arms stretched out as if he were "it" in a game of pin-the-tail on the donkey. Rheena ascended the stairs slowly, sliding her hand along the wall for both direction and comfort.

Ahead of her, the flashlight beam cast a spectral shadow on the wall. Zachary watched from the safety at the bottom of the stairs, straining his eyes as his sister disappeared into the dark hallway. Sudden bright flashes lit the street. They spilled through the window turning ordinary objects into odd shaped creatures.

"Wait!" Zachary cried out.

His voice bounced off the wall and returned unrecognizable to his ears. Bolstering his courage, Zachary ran the distance to the second floor just in time to see Rheena vanish through Papa's opened bedroom door and into the dark room. While Papa lived, this room had been his chamber. His cloudy eyes and empty pant leg chilled her. The end had been a quiet lingering, not sudden and unexpected like their father's. His high back chair, three months vacant, even now haunted the room.

In the top drawer, in the dresser beside the bed were the 15-amp fuses. In the closet Rheena knew she'd find the fuse box. The 10 feet from the door to the closet would take an eternity.

During the next blue flash of light, she located the closet, the dresser and the oak chair, its crushed velvet seat forever imprinted by a bony posterior. Adjacent to the chair, standing against the wall, bathed for an instant in the light, *ewe*.

Rheena steeled her nerve and determined to get to the fuses and to the fuse box in order to restore light to the house. She took a tentative step in the direction of the dresser, then another. The storm and her fear could be the only explanation for what happened next.

The floor shuddered under her stocking feet then was motionless again. Nor could she find a logical reason for the tilting of the room such that each step she took became more difficult. The beam from the flashlight threw an arch across the room swelling her shadow up the wall and on the floor behind her. She spun around quickly and saw the darkness again. In another flash she turned to see her brother framed by the door-jamb, his hands pressed for support against the frame.

"Rheena! What's going on?"

She thought he called to her from an impossible distance. Rheena reached the dresses in three swift steps. She pulled open the top drawer, and tucked beneath his socks, just as she had expected, were the fuses. The gray panel box in the closet was easy to locate with the flashlight. The colored knobs inside the box were marked with masking tape. Reena replaced the one where the penciled word *master* was scribbled, and the lamp by the bed flickered on. There wasn't much light, but it helped swallow up some of the darkness.

Outside, the lightning continued to flare, only now, the thunderous booms were missing. An eerie glow cascaded through the bedroom window. It flowed across the back of Papa's chair, and streamed like the rain, across the floor and onto ewe. The three of them, Rheena, Zachary and ewe, engulfed in the light and in the silence waited.

"When ewe ready to talk, he call to you." Rheena could hear Papa's sing-song voice echoing in her head.

Lightning flashed outside the window. With every flash, the call of ewe grew stronger. Zachary must have heard it too, because he eased closer to the drum, his hand extended as if to touch it. Was this what Papa meant? Was ewe calling?

Rheena looked from her brother's small brown hand to the profile of his face, barely visible in the dark, and to his hand again. Zachary wiggled his fingers then gave the drumhead a timid tap. The sound, however, that came forth was not a timid sound. It was a resounding boom!

Rheena jumped backward, startled. Her heel caught on the leg of Papa's high back chair and she sat down on the red cushion with a thump. The bedroom was once again quiet. They waited. When nothing untoward happened, she moved to the drum again.

She couldn't believe what she was doing. All of these weeks she had avoided this room. Emboldened, now she pulled the drum from its place by the wall. It was heavier than she had expected and it felt solid in her arms. Here they were; in Papa's room. In the dark of the storm, she held *ewe*, the talking drum.

The things in the room did not appear so frightening. She recalled how she and Zachary ran past the room chancing only a glance if the door was left ajar. Now, with the bedroom awash in the soft glow from the nightstand, she felt safe. The statues on the dresser, the smudged mirror, and the stacks of newspapers, books and magazines all rested harmlessly in their place. There was nothing frightening here. Even Papa's chair had lost its hair-raising hold on them.

Had they glanced back into the hallway, however, they would have noticed the rest of the house was still shrouded in darkness. The kitchen, the living room, dining room, their bedrooms, all cloaked in the blackness of the storm. Only Papa's bedroom was bathed in the eerie glow. But they never looked back. Their eyes were fixed on the talking drum

"Zachary, this is crazy!"

"I know. We're gonna get in trouble for touching Papa's drum," Zachary said without conviction.

"Do you feel like drumming?" she whispered.

Since the day they first discovered the drum, Zachary had wanted to play it. Now, at this odd time, the desire to drum overwhelmed him. He reached out once again. This time he let his hand rest on the drumhead. His palm rubbed in tiny circles, first one hand then the other.

"If I play, then you gotta dance," he insisted, his voice a whisper that failed to disguise his nervousness. Rheena nodded a slight jerk of her head. They were allies in this adventure so Rheena sat the drum down near her brother's feet.

Zachary offered another timid tap on the drum. The boom was an unexpected answer to the flash that momentarily illuminated the room. The two exchanged a nervous glance. Yet they had to continue. Zachary began to play with both hands, reluctant at first, the beat tentative, simple, an effortless rhythm that imitated the sound of footfalls. First one hand then the other, again and again.

When he was comfortable with this, he tried something more intricate. A tap, a pause; then, a quick alternation between each hand. With each strike, Zachary's palms seemed to push away from the goatskin drumhead. Gravity pulled his hands back down hard to have them pushed back up again. Before long, as if by charm, a rhythm was established and Zachary was lost in the experience. Papa had said he had the "gift."

Rheena rocked her body in place. For a while her feet rose just an inch or two off the worn red carpet that cover the bedroom floor. Then she began to lift her knees higher and higher with each step. She raised her arms like a bird about to take flight and bounced her shoulders up and down to the beat of her brother's drumming.

Through Papa's bedroom window the lightening flashed in concert with the playing as the distant thunder thrummed out a rhythm of its own.

Rheena turned her face to the ceiling. Her swaying arms now extended above her head. Her little brother played on, his eyes closed. They were having fun. More fun, in fact than any they had experienced since leaving Brooklyn. On and on Zachary drummed; faster and faster Rheena danced.

In a frenzy of motion, Rheena's body shimmied, her palms pushed through the air, elbows pointed out, double time to the left, double time to the right, above her head then down to her feet. Each knee, in turn lifting until it was almost waist high. The sequence of movement repeated again and again. It was no longer a thought of which step to take or which beat to create. The drum had taken over for the drummer and the dance had taken over the dancer. They had come out of the dance. Her feet moved of their own accord. His hands became a blur. Their sound became a lively celebration. Her arms stretched high into the air Rheena began to twirl in place. Her spin was slow at first; then, she turned faster and faster. Her movements, though dance like were becoming reckless and out of control. Overhead the ceiling fan swirled.

Then it happened. The ceiling began to spin. Each square tile circled counterclockwise overhead, each square following the next in a direction opposite to her. It was impossible, yet it was happening. Not only was the ceiling rotating, it was rising. Spiraling higher and higher away from Rheena's head. Taking with it the fan and the magazines, the statues, Papa's high back chair. Rheena was dizzy now. She was ready to fall down, to collapse to the floor, laughing with her brother as they made their way back downstairs to the kitchen. Rheena wanted to end the maddening dance. But the spinning continued despite her efforts to stop it.

Something held her fast. She had become the dance and could no more stop being than she could stop enjoying the feeling that her dance gave her. Had his eyes been open, Zachary might have seen his sister stumbling puppet-like around him. He might have witnessed the sky appearing overhead. His eyes, however, were shut tight, his head thrown back and swaying side to side. He saw nothing. But he heard … birds?

Over her head Rheena saw the morning doves take flight. She heard nightingales, blackbirds, chaffinches, -- and the voices. Rheena and Zachary both heard birds chirping and the murmurs of a crowd. And they both smelled the dry earthy dust that was being kicked up by Rheena's feet. They both felt the heat of the morning sun on their faces and the warm breeze that blew gently over their bodies. And they both felt a heavy hand grab them by the shoulders.

Zachary's eyes popped open as he fell back onto the dirt, landing hard on his bottom. In front of his face hung one of Papa's African ceremonial masks. The face dark and round. The maw near the bottom revealed yellow pick-like teeth.

"Eeeiiii!"

This horrifying sound came out of this gape in the mask at the mouth. Zachary made a sound of his own as he scrabbled backward in an effort to put distance between himself and the face that continued to float toward him. He kicked ewe and watched it roll across the dirt. He was outside and the storm was over.

"Eeeeiii!" The sound came again angrier than the first time.

"Wa chu doin', chile?"

The opening that was the mouth on the mask was moving. Before he could scream again, Zachary realized the mask was a face attached to a head, the head to a body. That somebody was speaking. Somebody grabbed him again. This time it was Rheena. She was poised mid-step and was using her brother's shoulder for balance. Her face distorted by her terror. She too saw this man with a face like an African mask.

"Rheena!" Zachary shouted.

"What happened?" Rheena's breath came in gasps.

"I …" he sputtered.

Then they heard the murmuring again. They dared to look around for the source of the voices, and saw the people. A crowd of about 30 or more men, women and children circled them. They were in an open yard. In the distance, giant oak trees towered. From the position of the sun and the sounds of the birdsongs, it was early morning.

The man with the face like an African ceremonial mask spoke again.

"Wah gwann?" he shouted at them in a hoarse whisper.

Frozen by their fear, Rheena and Zachary Mackey stared from their place on the ground at the African ceremonial mask face man that towered above. He beckoned with his arms and a circle of individuals from the crowd closed in around them. With a gesture, another stepped from the circle and moved with caution toward ewe.

"Leave it!" cried Rheena as she reached for Papa's drum. It had rolled a short distance from her brother and now rested near a dark man's bare foot. The circle fell back a step but moved in again even closer.

"*Don't let nobody get behind you!*" she heard Hoban shout in her head. "*Number four! Number four!*" Her brother's voice screamed in her mind. "*Rule #4*" it cried out "*Face out! Back to the wall!*"

But it was too late. At her back, a strong hand grabbed a fist full of her hair as powerful fingers clamped the back of her neck. From the front of her nightshirt Tweety Bird scowled at African mask face man. Rheena reached over her shoulders with both of her arms and twisted her body. She held fast to the wrist of her assailant. She winced as clumps of hair ripped from her scalp. Her nightshirt slid up revealing the *TGI Friday* smiley emoji on her yellow panties. The sight of the under garment that barely covered her exposed rump caused a gasp from the otherwise silent mob of onlookers. Furious, Rheena kicked backwards; scratched and clawed but to no avail. Her assailant's grasp was firm.

Beside her Zachary squirmed. His voice high and shrill.

"Lee me alone! Lemme go!" he screamed.

For an instant, Zachary freed himself from his captor and scrambled away on hands and toes like a terrified squirrel. A man's hand grabbed his foot but came away with only a white sock with blue stripes. The man studied the curious cloth seconds too long and Zachary pushed through the legs of the circle of startled onlookers and darted down the dirt road toward the dense forest of oak trees. He was quick; however, the legs of his pursuer were long. And the young man soon had a flailing Zachary hoisted under one arm like a sack of potatoes.

As one, the crowd pressed in even tighter. Rheena was spent. Zachary's ever-bountiful energy kept him grunting and punching, his useless blows landing in empty air.

"In nar!" the man with the face like an African mask commanded as he pointed to the door of a wooden shack. And the two children were tossed through the door landing hard onto the dirt floor. Zachary made one more attempt toward the door but was blocked by the same wily young fellow who had run him down. Held at arm's length as if it were something that he wanted neither to drop nor to touch him, he carried ewe which he placed with care in a corner on the far side of the room. He then grabbed up a handful of rags off of the dirt floor and covered the talking drum. It would be a long time before anyone ever saw it again.

6

Here We Are

RHEENA AND ZACHARY sat on the floor of the cabin in the dark. Even as the early morning light strained its way through the single curtain-less window they sat. The bulky man, with broad shoulders and the face of an African mask, was gone. He had pushed them inside, gawked at them for several long seconds then hurried out. A shorter, darker man carried *ewe* in behind them and secreted it under some rags in a corner. As this man scurried out of the dim into the daylight, he hastened Rheena and Zachary a quick glance, then he too was gone.

When the door opened next a woman came in. She was the only one, thus far, not in a hurry. She entered slowly, deliberately. She circled Rheena and Zachary like a cat studying a new toy. The woman was not very tall, but she was very large. Yards of dusty green fabric made up the long dress that covered her from neck to feet. An apron was wrapped around her considerable waist and ample bosom. Her oversized arms hung heavy away from her stout middle. She had a plump pleasant face that reminded Rheena of pancakes. Her hair was covered with a yellowing kerchief. At the nape of her neck peeked patches of wiry gray hair. And she was not smiling. Her pursed lips turned down at the corners. Her eyes, stark against her brown skin, watched them. She squinted first with one eye, then the other. Rheena's tummy rumbled. Zachary leaned closer to his sister.

The big woman stared long and hard, first at Zachary, then at Rheena. Her eyes finally came to rest on Tweety Bird. He alone did not flinch under the woman's glare. The big woman muttered something to herself. Then she spoke aloud, stretched out one plump arm and with a sharp flick of her head, nodded in the direction of the bench that flanked the table. The children did not understand anything she said. The gesture however was clear. They sprang from the floor and scrambled to the bench where they sat nearly on top of each other.

The big pancake face woman nodded her approval and began a slow purposeful walk round the room. She stopped in the corner where *ewe* was hidden, adjusted the clothes with her foot then strode past the two children and out the door.

Rheena and her little brother were alone. As their eyes adjusted to the dim, they could see the timber that was the walls and the ceiling. The floor underfoot was a yellowish brown hard-packed sandy loam. They were in a cabin. The flat-board table with benches on either long side where they sat hunched together took up most of the space. The only other place for sitting was a large wooden rocking chair near the bare window.

Rheena strained to see through the window by the door that was still ajar. She could see the motley crowd of people that moments earlier had been gathered around them. They now headed off purposefully in different directions. When she lifted herself up off the bench, she could see that, a short distance from the door, the large woman spoke with the big man. Her round face from time to time turned in their direction. After a while they too walked away.

Rheena and Zachary were all alone in the dim cabin. Inside it was like many of the Upstate New York wooden houses she and Hoban and Papa and Mama had spent summer afternoons in. Outside, however, things were different. The heat was different. It was a thick, wet, heavy heat. The people were different. The clothes they wore, old and worn. The smell was different, sweet and ocean salty rather than like the familiar pine needles and apples.

More important, they had been dancing in Papa's bedroom and now they were sitting in a strange cabin. *Ewe* had called to them. Rheena knew *ewe* was to blame for ... for whatever this was that had happened.

She peeled her arm from Zachary's shoulder and made her way to the window. Outside the sun had risen part way across the sky. It was well past breakfast. Her tummy rumbled again. She thought of the skillet of eggs she had left cooking on the stove. The flame lit under the pan of oil. When was that? Two hours ago? How long had they been sitting here? Here! Where was here?

Tears filled her eyes, brimmed over, and rolled down her cheeks. Tweety Bird watched defiantly out of the window from the front of her nightshirt, her tears wetting Tweety's big blue eyes. Why had she not learned to obey? *"... get some cold cereal. Don't turn on the stove!!!"* Mama's note had read. *"Hoban, fix your brother and sister something hot for breakfast. I'll be back by one. Love, Mom."*

This was all Hoban's fault, Rheena thought. Had he been home like he was supposed to be he would have fixed their eggs. He would have checked the fuse box when the power went out. They never would have had to go into Papa's bedroom. She and Zachary would not have played and danced with *ewe* in Papa's bedroom. They would not be here. Where?

"Papa's kitchen must be on fire by now," she thought. The house ... their home, burning down. Probably already burned to the ground. *"Nobody in! Nobody out!"* Mama had written. When Mama returned home at one clock, she would find them gone and the house burned down.

"If Hoban were here, he'd know exactly what to do," Rheena thought. She missed her big brother. She missed her mother. No, this was not Hoban's fault. Rheena knew that. "Nobody in! Nobody out!" They were definitely out.

Rheena turned from the window to examine the cabin. Zachary was already up and walking around. His hand skimmed along the horizontal wooden beams that were the walls. His eyes explored from dirt floor to thatched ceiling. His foot kicked curiously at the blankets stacked in neat folds on the dirt floor. A wicker work basket stuffed with colorful scraps of fabric, spools of threads, and two scissors stood nearby. Zachary peered into the basket and pulled out what looked to be a bed quilt that someone was still working on. A pair of iron scissors clattered to the dirt floor. He grabbed up the scissors and pushed the quilt along with the scissors back into the basket and continued his investigation.

There it was. The pile of fabric under which was hidden the talking drum. Zachary squatted in front of the rags, his finger gently peeling back the first layer of cloth. Rheena watched.

"Rheena, maybe we should do it again," he whispered as he moved the first cover.

"We can put things back the way they were." He prepared to move more of the cloths.

"Dun' tush dat!" a voice hissed from behind them.

Zachary and Rheena jumped and turned in one startled motion. It was the big woman. She was back. Her hoarse shout frightened Rheena and Zachary back to the table.

The big woman was not empty handed. From one hand dangled a steaming black kettle. With her other hand, she clutched two bowls against her body. Hurriedly, she dropped the pot down hard onto the table. The pad that wrapped around the hot iron handle and protected her hand from the heat fell inside the kettle. The big woman rushed, bowls in hand, across the room to where *ewe* was hidden. She squatted effortlessly for her size, pushed the covers back into the corner, pat them in several places and she stood up. A long slow sigh of relief whistled from between her pursed lips.

She came back to the table, her face awash in a toothy smile. Rheena thought of waffles, with melted butter and strawberries.

Instead, the big woman had brought a deliciously smelling pot of stew. After cautiously retrieving the potholder from inside the kettle where it had fallen, she ladled the mixture of beans and bits of meat into the bowls. All the while she chortled a sing-song gibberish that neither Rheena nor her brother understood. From her apron pocket the big smiling woman offered two wooden spoons, one spoon for each of them.

Anxiety and hunger battled in their stomachs for their attention. Hunger won. Rheena and Zachary ate greedily, even the bits of meat. When the wooden spoons scrapped the bottom of the bowls the big woman filled them again.

When the bowls emptied a second time, the big woman took up the ladle, the empty kettle, the bowls, and the spoons and left the two children alone again. They watched her through the open door as she walked away from the cabin. Then they turned to stare at the corner where the talking drum was hidden. If they were going to chance doing another dance, they would have to be alone.

Emboldened by a full belly the two children went to the open cabin door. The sun was nearly overhead. The air was still. Rheena ventured a few timid steps outside. Her brother followed close behind her. Except for the bird songs, and the distant sound of a deep voice singing a low sad song, it was quiet. No one was around. Four more steps and they were out in the open. They looked around. Still, they could see no one. They could see nothing that was familiar.

Overhead the sun burned hot, so Rheena and Zachary sought the shade of a nearby cabbage palmetto tree and crouched down. They sheltered beneath the branches of the palmetto tree near a well-worn path that disappeared in both directions. Several buildings, more shanty than cabin like the one they had been thrown into, lined both sides of the road. When they leaned forward and looked in either direction, they could see that the path branched off into additional dirt paths. Zachary's small voice broke the silence.

"Rheena, remember when we used to go with Hoban and Mama to the Beaverkill?"

He watched over his sister's shoulder; his eyes focused on something he viewed in the distant. Rheena's eyes began to sting as she fought back the tears that suddenly threatened her vision. Until now, the children had not spoken out loud of their mother or their older brother or anything else that might remind them of the hopelessness of their situation.

"Yeah," she answered.

"Remember," he continued his voice barely above a whisper, "how Hoban found that beaver that time and we argued about whether a beaver and a badger were the same thing?"

"Yeah."

Vivid memories flooded Rheena's mind of the two of them running and screaming as their older brother chased them with the decayed carcass of a long dead animal. Somehow, he'd managed to hook it on a tree branch. Mama called for Hoban to stop. Each time he would say: "Sorry, okay. I'm sorry."

When they calmed down, he would raise the stick at them and set off the barrage of shrieking and screaming anew. Throughout the day, long after Shirley and Hoban had buried the dead animal, he would shake an object, a paper plate, his wet swim trunks, anything at hand and yell: "Oh, no! It's back!" and the two children, to Shirley Mackey's bemused dismay, would resume their screeching.

"And remember," he continued, "that silly badger picture that Hoban drew and would show me and make me cry?"

A heavy lump rose in Rheena's chest. That silly cartoon drawing that her older brother had created caused such distress in Zachary, that for years they had only to mention it and it would bring him to tears.

"I know you're not still scared of that old picture!" she ventured.

"No. I'm not. I was just a kid then."

Rheena fought back her tears. She marveled at how bravely her little brother was dealing with their dilemma.

"Why do you ask," she whispered.

"Do you remember what it looked like?" he continued. Rheena nodded.

"Well, don't turn around," Zachary said, "but this guy coming looks just like Hoban's badger."

Rheena suppressed the urge to turn around and look at whomever her brother was watching. *Don't turn around* was a game that could keep the Mackey family entertained for days. It relieved tension in the most awkward of situations. This time, however, it was too painful to play. But if it helped her brother deal, she would play.

She maneuvered in her spot on the ground until she could tactfully see who was approaching. She could hear dragging footfalls and could tell by how Zachary pulled his focus that someone was drawing near. Apparently, Zachary was not going to scream and Rheena's heart ached. She imagined her mother and older brother in a frantic search throughout what was left of the house and moving door to door through the neighborhood shouting for them to answer.

"Hi," Zachary said when a shadow fell across the ground in front of them.

Rheena turned around and looked up, and just as Zachary had predicted, there above them stood a man who remarkably resembled the cartoon badger Hoban had drawn. His oval face was the color of khaki. His eyes, mere slits, were balanced on top of a pug nose. Sandy red hair formed thousands of beads atop a head that joined the neck and blended into hunched shoulders that appeared to be made of melted wax. The image of the badger made both Zachary and Rheena want to scream and run. But where would the run to?

"Hi, back at ya!" he said. And for the first time the children heard words that were familiar.

"You speak English." Rheena was pleased.

"Course." The answer was simple. "Wha' chu spec?"

"Everyone else sounds so.... We can't understand anything anyone says," Rheena explained.

"Well, gal. You sho soun' funny t'all us."

"I suppose so," Rheena conceded.

"Wont ya'll t' kno' rations been gib out all ready," he said.

"I don't understand," she said.

"Ev'a Sa'ti'dee dey gibs all us seben daysa ration. Seben days meal, seben daysa beans, seben daysa dry meats. Brownridge tells us we gotta share, counta he ain't figu'd wha'ta do 'bout two yous." He raised one dusty eyebrow to advise them of his meaning. His implication was not clear to them. They still didn't understand. The man took in a breath, exhaled, and spoke again. His address slower, words were more measured.

"'counta you two, a body gon' be hungry comes next ration day." He paused. "What wit' two mouths mo'."

Rheena thought of the two bowls of beans with bits of meat she and her brother had consumed earlier. She felt just a little guilty that someone might have to do without because of them. The beans had been delicious and eating the meat was not as bad as she had expected it would be. The big woman had brought the food to them. She had offered them the food.

"That big lady gave us the food," Rheena protested.

"Besides, we were hungry," Zachary added. The man's faced puckered into a smile.

"Dat big lady Aint Zori. Aint Zori, she luvs da chi'ren!"

"We won't be here that long," Rheena muttered. The man that resembled a badger turned his head on his pudgy neck and looked about, fearful that someone might overhear their conversation.

"Talk lak dat git ya a heap a troubles," his reply guarded.

"Can't we ask for our own rations," Zachary stated rather than asked. The badger snorted a sound that was intended as a laugh.

"Aks Brownridge? He jest the driver," the Badger said, derision dripping from his tone. "…'signs tasks, dats 'bout all." He puckered his lips and spat out a puff of air.

"We don't want anyone to suffer because of us." Rheena tried to sound grown-up.

There must be an easy solution to this situation that the man they came to refer to as the Badger was obviously not able to think of. Everything that had happened so far was unusual. If it was unusual for her and Zachary, she could only imagine how it must be for everyone else. How often do a boy and a girl and a drum appear out of thin air. Rheena was certain that that is what ewe had caused to happen.

"Who do we talk to about more rations?" She spoke in her most adult voice.

"Dat be da ov'a see'a. He a mean'un, dat." The Badger pursed his lips and shook his head from side to side. Rheena and Zachary waited for the man to finish shaking his head and offer a solution of his own.

"Maybe we he'p owa se'ves," he finally said.

"Help ourselves! You mean steal?" Now it was Rheena's turn to look guardedly around. She was met with the unreadable face of the Badger.

"Folks be sleepin' 'fore long," he continued.

"Let me get this straight!" But she already had it straight and she knew she did.

"Massa got plenty. Folks be sleepin' 'fore long. We he'p owa se'ves," he said as he walked off with a slow badger waddle. He had made up his mind.

Without streetlights, darkness descended quick and thorough. The two children watched from the safety of the palmetto tree as the people entered the shanties that lined both side of the dirt road. They were nearest Ain't Zori's place and since it was the place where the talking-drum was hidden, by silent and mutual agreement Rheena and Zachary sought night shelter there.

7

The Discovery

INSIDE AINT Zori's cabin, Rheena and Zachary found six or more children in various areas of the cozy room already snoring on pallets. A lantern sat in the middle of the table. The flame threw an orange glow across the single room.

"Tek dis." Aint Zori's voice came from the dark. Her ample arms extended two woolen blankets and a hand full of sacks to them. She pointed to an empty spot on the floor and the two children, obedient more to fatigue than her directions, prepared for bed and quickly crumpled under the itchy blankets.

For a long while they lay in silence. They stared into the dark. Tears pooled in Zachary's ears and Rheena pulled him close to her. Before long he fell asleep.

Rheena watched Aint Zori, who sat in the wooden rocking chair in the dim light sewing and humming a wordless tune. A night sound, like the whistling of a small bird, cut through her song and caught her attention. She put aside her sewing and pushed her brawny self up from the seat of the chair. Taking up the lantern from the center of the table she went outside, quietly closing the cabin door.

The room was plunged into darkness. Rheena stared into the black at the rectangle where the door had been. From beyond it she could hear the muffled conversation in the strange tongue she and Zachary had listened to all this first day. It droned on and soon her lids grew heavy.

"Gal! Gal!" Rheena heard a vaguely familiar voice whispering out. She opened her eyes to the darkness. She was on the bridge of a battle-damaged starship. Somehow, she had been beamed aboard and was out of breath from running through corridors and passageways, looking for the access that would lead her to the vehicle her father had parked in the driveway. She reached a wall. There, she pressed her left shoulder so hard against the partition she believed was an exit panel, her arm became numb.

"Gal!" The whispered call came again. Rheena drifted up from that magical sleep state and realized that she had been dreaming. She opened her eyes, expecting to see through the window overlooking Papa's flower garden. Instead, her face pressed against the hard surface beneath her. Her left arm was stiff, and she was unable to move it. Rheena tried to turn over and climb up out of bed when she realized she was on the floor. Gradually, it came to her. This must be another part of her dream.

Zachary lay snoring, his head tucked snug in the crook of her left arm. They lay on a dirt floor in a strange cabin in a strange place.

Around her she could hear the exhausted breathing of ten or more small children.

"Gal!" The whisper was louder now. This was no dream. Someone was calling from the door.

In the moonlight that filtered through the window Rheena recognized the man she and her brother had nicknamed the Badger. She slipped her arm, numbed from where it rested, from beneath her brother's head. In his sleep, Zachary mumbled some unintelligible words then laughed. She was glad for him. His dream seemed to be a pleasant one. Rheena crawled across the floor so as not to step on any of the other sleepers who snored and grunted in their slumber. She pulled open the door letting in the night air.

"Psst!"

Just outside the door the Badger, with a jerk of his head, signaled her to join him. She feared leaving Zachary and the drum, but so far, this one was the only one here whose speaking she could understand. If this were still a dream, perhaps she could get some answers for when she woke up.

The Badger carried a lantern trimmed low, and other than the pale light of the moon, she had only the soft sound of his breathing to guide her. He set a brisk pace as he walked up ahead. Rheena was still wearing her Tweety Bird nightshirt and the cool night air on her bare legs made her teeth chatter. She thought of all of the safeguards Hoban would have for her. But she needed answers and this one was obviously more interested in where he was going than in whom he was going there with.

She followed several steps behind him down the dirt road that separated the two rows of wooden and thatched shanties until they came to a structure longer than the others. The building was set back farther from the road and had the words *storehouse* painted with bold white letters on the side.

The Badger double-stepped around the building's far end where two large stones lay on the ground. One of the stones leaned against the foundation and blended with the dirt and rocks that circled the storehouse. When Rheena caught up with him he gestured for her to take the lantern. The warm handle in her hand added a measure of comfort to her, but not enough to stay the shiver that skipped through her body.

His hand now free, the Badger lifted the larger of the stones, which allowed a piece of wood to free itself a bit from against the wall. A slight tug and the wood slanted to reveal a hole just large enough for him to crawl through. He lowered himself to his knees, took the lantern and deftly slid into the opening. Seconds later his hand re-appeared and beckoned Rheena to do the same. She dropped to her knees and with caution, poked her head into the opening. Wooden panels on both sides limited her view of the space. Above her head, more wood. Up ahead, she could see the floor bathed in the receding lantern light. To continue, she would have to pull her body through this tight confinement and into whatever awaited. Steeling her resolve Rheena belly crawled forward.

Twice, her hair snagged on the low ceiling, but after a short distance of a few feet, she was clear. Squatting close to the floor she looked around. The interior of the storehouse was enormous. She realized the hidden opening through which she had just crawled was the sides of crates, the plank above had been the underside of shelves. Rheena racked her fingers through her matted hair and surveyed the inside of the storehouse.

Shelves lined the far wall, as well as the wall at her back. On these platforms, stacked almost to the ceiling, burlap sacks bulged from their content. In the center of the room she counted fifteen wooden barrels. The waist high containers belted with black metal were in two straight rows. The Badger was already busy scooping into the sacks that until now had been concealed under his shirt, the contents of the barrels marked in black with the words beans, cornmeal, flour and rice.

Rheena took the lantern from the floor at the Badger's feet and held it high overhead to better see the interior of the storehouse and to watch him at work. He grunted his thank you and with an open hand, shoved his arm elbow deep into the center of the barrel of butter beans. When he removed a fist filled with the barrel's content the surface appeared undisturbed. Nothing spilled out. Even as he closed one sack, his feral eyes were fixed on the next barrel he would open. Rheena was certain he had done this many time before. She lighted the way along the line of barrels. With her there to assist he worked swiftly. Soon more than 10 small sacks were tied to a rope and slung over the Badger's shoulders.

It was at the end of the second long row that Rheena discovered the desk. It was a smaller version of the plank in the cabin but without the flanking benches, that someone used as a writing table. She walked behind the wooden chair that had been pushed in place. And there, on the floor, beside the chair, caught for an instant in the flicker of the lantern light, lay a gold coin. It positioned as if it had fallen and had not yet been missed. Rheena's heart leapt in her chest.

She placed the lantern on the table and sidestepped until she could feel the shape of the metal beneath her foot. She scrunched her toes, waited, and then stepped away from the table. The Badger glanced at her before resuming his confiscation, taking just enough, then smoothing his fingertips over the indent that was left so that the content looked uninterrupted. He moved to the next barrel.

Rheena lifted her foot. Balancing on one leg, she pretended to remove a pebble or similar object from her sock. Her trembling hand palmed the gold coin; her arms resting at her sides. When her hands stopped shaking, she folded the coin in to a bunch of fabric at her waist. She would forgo its examination for a more discreet opportunity. The Badger seemed not to have taken notice, so she continued her investigation of the makeshift desk.

Arranged on one side of the tabletop were a brown leather book, a bottle of black ink and a brown gold flecked fountain pen. Rheena raised the lantern for better light. The fingers of her free hand tapped along the surface of the desk until they reached the book. Her fingertips traced the fancy script written across the face of the book: Hammond Plantation Beaumont South Carolina. She mouthed the words as she read. She squinted, leaned in closer and read the words again. Plantation. Rheena began to tremble much more than the night air warranted. Without thought of consequences, she gripped the edge of the book and lifted open the long brown cover. The first page identified the book and its owner: Orin Beauchamp. Underneath the carefully scrawled words she read: ledger 1848.

Rheena flipped to the next page. It was marked: bought. There were three columns. One headed *item*, one headed *amount*, and the third headed *date*. She slid her finger down the page muttering out loud each word as she came to it.

Flour 100 pounds ten dollars; 2 bolts coarse grain fabric / 20 dollars; 1 pair male Negroes / $100; 3 five-pound barrels of molasses … the list went on. Rheena could not.

She glanced up at the Badger. Though intent on what he was doing, his beady eyes watched her warily. Rheena turned in place, wide eyed, taking in everything she could see in the large space. Folded neatly on the shelves were shirts and trousers of all sizes, skirts, and bonnets, like the ones she saw earlier. Standing in order against the wall was row upon row of boots. Some were tiny, others grown man size. A rush of adrenaline filled her stomach.

What had she experienced earlier? So many Black men and women working, barefoot children, strong Gullah sing-song patter like her grandfather's; the people with downcast eyes.

Now she began to understand. Papa had warned them many times: *"It be a magical ting!"* Ewe, the talking drum, had brought them here. Transported them to Beaumont, South Carolina, the bondage place of her grandfather's ancestors. If this were true, she and her brother Zachary were not only thousands of miles from Monticello, New York, but tens of decades as well.

Rheena wanted to run. But run to where? Her mind began to recall the cruel stories of slavery and plantation life. She wished, too late, that she had paid better attention to the things her Papa had spoken about, to the movies and television specials her parents had forced them to watch so that they "would know." Because, if what she suspected, however impossible, were true, ... they were lost in time, a long way from home and in grave danger.

A powerfully unpleasant feeling of dread ran through her. What if she and the Badger were caught? Stealing from the plantation storehouse! What if the Badger had noticed that she had been reading the words in the leather brown book? Reading by slaves had been against the law. Punishable by who knew what means. Her only thoughts now were to leave this frightful place. Take the lantern and go quickly to her brother. Find the drum, play and dance until the awful instrument reworked its magic and carried them back north; carried them back to Monticello; carried them back to their time.

She looked once again at the open book, at the list of names and the numbers and the dollar amounts on the page.

"Get out!" a voice screamed in her head.

She slammed the ledger shut and staggered across the floor; past the Badger, whose arms were laden with foodstuff.

"Let's go!" she said out loud, more calmly than she felt. He obeyed.

The Badger took the lantern and the two of them crawled back under the shelf, through the opening and into the night. He replaced the stone, then kicked the loose soil about to conceal their footprints. Rheena followed his lead down the road past dark and silent cabins.

At Aint Zori's door the Badger slowed down with the lantern. He kept all of the food. Without shame, Rheena squatted on the ground and emptied her bladder. The man she called the Badger quickly disappeared into the dark night.

Inside Rheena found Zachary, still asleep. A frown creased his brow. She sat beside him. Wrapping her arms around her bent knees, she rocked, the gold coin gently tapping her side. Rheena stared in the direction of the door until she heard a rooster heralding the start of the new day.

Sometime during the night, she was not sure if it was before or after her discovery with the Badger, Aint Zori returned. As the cock crowed, Aint Zori went about making a fire in the great stove. It wasn't long before the sounds of early risers began to fill the cabin. Not everyone got up quickly. Rheena wanted to use the bathroom. She thought of how desperately she wanted to shower and wondered what she could find to wear.

Her little brother stretched beside her and opened his eyes. He looked first surprised and then disappointed.

"I thought I was dreaming," he moaned.

"Go outside and pee with the others," Rheena advised. Zachary followed the other children who stumbled out half asleep to the outhouse that stood a safe distance from the cabin.

"Fount dis." Aint Zori extended her arms, which held several garments that Rheena soon identified as bloomers, a skirt, and a blouse. They were large but she slipped them on over her nightshirt. The boots were snug over her socks so she removed the socks, knotted them together and used them to tie her hair in place.

The old Black woman watched with interest as Rheena dressed, slipped on the boots, and tied up her hair. It seemed that the old Black woman expected her assistance. So, after her turn in the outhouse and splashing water on her face and under her arms, Rheena joined Aint Zori by the cook fire.

Aint Zori stirred the contents of a three-legged iron kettle that stood inside the massive stone oven that covered one entire wall. There was no toaster, no microwave, or gas oven. And after much mixing, kneading, and frying, the two had a meal of biscuits, sausages and gravy to feed a cabin full of hungry boys and girls who seemed to appear from every direction to fill every corner of the room.

The mood of the encampment was considerably more jovial than when they arrived the day before. Most of the children seemed to pay no attention to the Mackey children. Someone, perhaps Aint Zori, had given Zachary a pair of pants and a shirt and he too wore boots, inches too long for his feet.

"Zach, you better sit down and eat," Rheena suggested.

She decided to wait until they were fed and alone before sharing with her brother what she'd discovered the night before.

They would locate the magic drum and test it. They would play it and dance until they were safe back home. If escaping from slavery was the other option from which they had to choose, they needed a plan. If time followed true, then today was Sunday. And certainly, even on a Southern plantation, Sunday was a day of rest. Perhaps they could find time to plan their getaway.

Breakfast was more leisurely than the meals the day before and Aint Zori told one little boy that tugged at her apron:

"Fo troot. T'dees off-dee."

As each child filled their belly, they quickly ran from their eating area and disappeared outside the door. Zachary finished his plate of biscuits, eggs and beans and looked at his sister for direction.

"Stay nearby," Rheena whispered. "We gotta talk."

Zachary nodded his understanding of the importance of her words then followed the others out of doors. Several older boys brought buckets of water to the cabin then raced out the door assigning their shouts to the shouts of the others. Soon the area was humming with the squeals of children at play.

In short order, Rheena and Aint Zori had washed the dishes and broom-swept the cabin floor. When they were nearly done, a little doe-eyed boy toddled back into the cabin interrupting them with his crying. Cooing words of comfort, Aint Zori whisked him into her ample arms. She wiped the water that stained his cheeks and trickled down his legs then shooed him back outside. When he was gone, she laughed a deep rich laugh and chattered a funny story in her strange Gullah patter inviting Rheena with her smile to laugh along with her. To Rheena's surprise, it wasn't long before she was able to pick up snatches of familiar sounds from her words. Translating them into words that she knew.

When the cleanup was done and the broom rested in its place beside the hearth, Aint Zori started for the door. She hung her apron on the nail near the broom. Then as an afterthought, she turned and looked at Rheena.

"Spec Brownridge figguh 'bout yu," she said before leaving Rheena alone in the cabin.

Rheena turned in place, searching. Beside the neatly stacked sleeping pallets, in a dark corner, she found it. Secreted beneath a pile of Aint Zori's sewing cloth waited ewe.

8

The Arrival

IT WAS SATURDAY, though most of the people on the Hammond Plantation at Redcliff didn't care to name the day. The name of the day was determined by the tasks of the day. Plow-day, washday, row-day, candle-day, clod-day, dry-day, seed-day, weed-day, every-day until all the soiled clothes were clean clothes day, the vegetables came up in rows in the small garden plots day, and the rice seedlings grew taller than a man day.

Most days these task-days overlapped, giving the same 24 hours two, sometimes three or four, day-names. Many times, named day was repeated several times during a week. It was up to Brownridge to name the day and assign the tasks. No day mattered to the people more than off-day. This day was not off-day. It was Saturday. And every able body and many who were not very able in body were already stitching, hoeing, shoeing or sloshing in the boot top high waters of the rice field. It was early this April Saturday morning when they first heard the sounds.

Far into the distance, it rumbled. Like an approaching storm, it rolled. There had been no indication from the insects, or the smells in the air or from aching joints that a storm was expected. Most thought the deep grumbling that came out of nowhere, but was felt everywhere, was thunder. Several who slaved in the murky water chanced a nervous glance up into the cloudless morning sky. They knew, should it rained now, the water would flood the rice fields too soon. Should it storm now, bolts of lightning could zig-zag through the air to strike anyone standing, as many were, in the open.

All of a sudden came the ear-piercing thwack! Followed immediately by a terrifying rumble. Stunned, the slaves froze, fixed in place. Some remained bent at their task; while others slowly straightened, prepared to react. Each looked to the person nearest them to determine that they were not alone, they looked up into the clear, blue sky.

Then the unexpected happened. The earsplitting rip, crash, boom; a brief pause, and another boom threw everyone to the ground. The silence that followed was more deafening than the original thunderclap. The loud, ground-shaking noise resumed. It continued for too many heartbeats.

Brownridge was the first to move. He squared his big broad shoulders and began a desperate gallop across the stream and in the direction of the Quarters. The little brown and Black children also began to frantically sprint for the safety of the quarters. Emboldened, the others followed. Some of the men and women were able to keep up with the big, Black man. The others, laden by the huge baskets filled with seeds strapped across their shoulders, moved with more effort.

At the living quarters, running over from every direction, more slaves began to gather as the thunderous sounds morphed into rhythmic beats. The people clustered together, murmuring in fear and confusion at what they could hear but could not see. It was a rhythm that had not been heard in these parts for many, many decades. It was a forbidden sound. It was the sound that both excited and incited. It was for those reasons it was forbidden. It was the drum beat of their motherland, of Africa.

Without warning, the source of the African drumming appeared. Out of the nothingness there materialized in the form of an oddly clad little brown boy who thumped to the ground onto his bottom in front of the stunned crowd. A small ewe clenched between his knees, his eyes closed, his head thrown back, the boy appeared. His hands moved in a flurry of motion creating patterns of sounds that moments before was thought to be thunder. As one, the crowd gasped and fell back at the sudden manifestation.

Before the people could further react, again from the nothingness, appeared flailing arms and legs. A brown girl danced. It was a rhythm and a dance that many of the people had heard tell of from a time and a place long gone. Now they were both eye and earwitness to it. The crackling had stopped but the drumming continued. The people in the back of the crowd pushed forward to get a better view.

Wrestling his fear aside, Brownridge muscled his way through the cloud of dust and dirt that rose into the air around the two children.

"Eeeiiii," he cried.

His hands trembled as he reached toward the apparitions that continued to move. It would not do for the people to see how terrified he was. He readied to strike the two down if need be.

"Wa chu doin', chile?" he cawed in his bravest voice. He had to stop them. This thing they did was forbidden. Then one of the two spoke a sound he could not understand.

"Rheena!" the drummer sang out.

"Wah gwann?" Brownridge shouted back in a hoarse whisper.

The small boy's drumming stopped and the small girl's dancing, after a few more staggering steps also ceased. Brownridge slapped a trembling hand onto the shoulder of the dancer. She was small; however, she was incredibly strong and wiry. He held her up off the ground by the scruff of the neck like a captured fox. She fought back just as viciously. Several times the two nearly escaped. However, he and his man were stronger and faster. And just as swiftly as they had appeared the two were hurried into the nearest cabin. The drum, which lay discarded in the dirt, was carried in as well.

At the top of the bluff, a terrified Orin Beauchamp lay on the ground watching the commotion amongst the slaves down below.

9

The Overseer

ORIN BEAUCHAMP woke from a fitful night's sleep to the distant sound that thundered in his skull. Once again, his head ached. This time the pain had the regularity of a drumbeat. Not the tatter-tatter tat of the marching drum, but the incessant thundering that he recalled from his boyhood of the African drumming that the slaves were now forbidden to do.

The cargo ship from the Bahamas to America's South heading north for New Brunswick, Canada, was due in soon. As far as Orin Beauchamp was concerned, it could not dock soon enough. He enjoyed smoking the special herbs that the captain aboard had and was willing to sell to him. With just a few pinches remaining, he had taken to mixing it with tobacco; however, that mixture was without the same peaceful enjoyment he felt when he smoked the ganja on its own. His supply of tobacco was also low. And these simple pleasures made the unbearable responsibility of overseeing Hammond Plantation tolerable.

The heat from the sun and the wet sticky mist that rolled in from the swamp drove his brother, Jean Michel, and the rest of the family inland to their Georgia Estate at Redcliffe. Most of the time Orin wished he could strike out on his own. Night and day, he dreamed of going West to dig for gold; of going into Indian Territory where the wilderness and the unknown of the frontier had to be better than slaving here amongst these ungodly Blacks from Africa. But he stayed behind in order to insure his inheritance.

He understood nothing about these primitives or their ways. He never understood when they spoke. He never understood how they tolerated the heat or the backbreaking work. He always wondered when they would realize that he was outnumbered. That he was a hapless one against their countless number. Thinking about it frightened him; it exhausted him. And he must never let them know that. He was one to their many. So, he kept control by keeping them more afraid of him than he was of them. That took all the meanness he had in him. It took his legendary skill with the bullwhip that always hung by his side

He hated that he needed his slave driver, Brownridge. The big Black brute translated everything. When something needed to be done, he told Brownridge and Brownridge told the Blacks. He was as much a slave to them as they were to him. But the work got done. It was not a perfect system, but it was a system that worked.

As soon as he got enough provisions, he was leaving this god-awful place. Folks would look for him and he'd be gone. Headed west.

Let his brother find someone else to oversee the rice planting, harvesting, and selling.

The thundering beat that woke him continued even after he'd opened his eyes. The sun, already above the horizon, poked a narrow yellow beam through the cloth that hung as a curtain. Beauchamp stumbled through the door of his two-room sleeping space and outside into the morning. He sighed with relief as he emptied his full bladder against the rocks at his feet. Yet, the pounding beat continued.

A half empty bottle of corn liquor lay on the ground near the toe of his boot. He retrieved it, turned it up to his mouth and took in a big swig, swished it around in his mouth and spat it out. The clattering grew louder. Beauchamp turned to face the ruckus that came from over the bluff in the direction of the slave quarters.

In the distance down below, something was kicking up a cloud of dusty earth. The ball of earth, which grew in size, seemed animated. Out of the cloud of noise and dirt there appeared a pair of arms, then another; legs, and arms and hair flailed in all directions. Orin rubbed his eyes with his knuckles, squinted and made another attempt to pull focus. A small knot of the slaves was gathering. The sound must be originating from them. He ticked off the days of the week with his fingers against his thigh. It was Saturday. There was still work to be done. They were allowed to congregate on Sunday but not on Saturday. Even then, only hand clapping and foot stomping was allowed. No drumming.

If it didn't stop soon, he'd have to grab his bullwhip, ride down there and put a stop to it. He spotted Brownridge's broad shoulders in the crowd. Good. Brownridge would handle this ruckus and he would handle Brownridge later for allowing the commotion in the first place. Brownridge was bending over one of the two young 'uns. That one was the cause of the racket. It was too far away to make out which young'un it was.

Then, suddenly, she appeared. Out of thin air into the settling dust, arms whirling and flapping, she appeared. How had he not seen her before? Orin Beauchamp frowned. She was there, all right. His eyes might be tricking him. But there she was. Plain as day, jumping and thrashing like they used to do on Sunday years ago when his daddy was still alive and had to put a stop to it. Beside her was another one. Maybe one of them was having a fit. If either one was sick, he'd have to get rid of it. Sell it. Maybe even kill it before it spread whatever it had to the others. He needed a better look.

Orin hurried back inside the tiny cabin to get his spyglass. He used the glass to watch the slaves from above without having to mount up and ride down below amongst them. He kept it on the shelf beside his bed. But now that he needed the spyglass, he could not locate it. This was the second thing he had lost in as many days.

The night before, Orin Beauchamp had franticly tossed his few possessions around the two rooms in a fruitless search for his missing gold coin. When he lifted the pile of dirty shirts and soiled long johns as he hunted for the coin, he heard the spyglass roll across the floor and under the chest of drawers. Had he stopped then to retrieve it, he would have it now. But he hadn't stopped; his search for the missing gold coin, finding the coin was more important. He never found the coin, and had fallen asleep exhausted from too much drink, frustration and fist pounding.

Now he lay belly down on the cabin floor scrapping his arm back and forth under the chest of drawers willing his fingers to touch the instrument. One more sweep of his fingers against the floor and he managed to tap an edge of the glass. All the while, the thundering beat outside grew louder.

Finally, with the magnifier in hand, he scurried across the floor and out the door. Beauchamp planted himself on the brush and peered down once again toward the slave quarters. Beside him a killdeer screamed her protest as his hand strayed too near her nest. Overhead a woodpecker tapped out a warning. Abruptly, the drumming stopped. It was morning quiet again. Beauchamp strained, the spyglass pressed to one eye to see, to hear. No more sound came from the quarters below. The two children were also gone. The crowd of slaves dispersed. And in the silence, he was no longer sure that there had ever been anything to see.

10

Sunday

SUNDAY MORNING was a day of rest on the Hammond Plantation. Situated in the doorway of the cabin, Rheena could see that most of the Blacks were dressed in what had to be their Sunday best, not in the dull gray and brown coarse cloth of the day before. From beneath the hems of the long skirts worn by the women, peeked bits of white linen gathered into ruffles. Scarves and bonnets covered their neatly combed hair. The men pulled their suspenders on as they piled into the backs of the mule-drawn wagons that kicked up dust as they rolled casually down the road. Behind a cabin someone tilled the soil around a new garden. Others carried pails and walked with fishing poles slung over their shoulders. The laughter of children filled the air as they ran about in play.

Rheena searched the bustling crowd of strangers for Aint Zori or even the African mask face man that both Aint Zori and the Badger had referred to as Brownridge. She thought she recognized the Badger's familiar outline in the figure of the man who was slinking away from the others, heading off through the distant tree line. Two dead chickens lolled from a strap draped around his neck. His back bent under the burden of several bulging burlap sacks strung together across his shoulders. Rheena saw no one else she could identify.

"Rheena!"

Zachary's familiar voice called from across the way. Zachary Mackey blended so thoroughly with the other Black children that she barely recognized him. He raced toward her followed by two who appeared a few years older than herself.

"Meet my new friends," Zachary called out as he hurried toward his big sister. "This is Annie Peavey and this is Piper," he said indicating first the cream-colored teenage girl and then the coal dark young man.

Annie strode several bold steps up to Rheena and walked a slow circle around her. Through squinted eyes she examined her face, her hair, and Rheena's ill-fitting clothes. Zachary could not contain his amusement.

"They think you're a haint," he chuckled.

"A what?"

"A haint. That's like a ghost in their language." Zachary giggled some more, but Piper and Annie remained cautious.

"I'm no ghost!" Rheena protested.

"That's what I keep telling them," her little brother said.

Piper appeared to be about their brother Hoban's age and stood about the same height. A rucksack hung at his side; its wide strap stretched on a diagonal crossed his broad chest. He kept his gaze focused on the ground but stole glances at Rheena and Zachary when—

ever they looked away from him. Annie was more direct with her investigation. She was especially fascinated by Rheena's nightshirt and the bold yellow bird that scowled out at the world from behind an open button on her blouse.

"My daddy gave it to me," Rheena said clutching her blouse closed. "He says I'm just like Tweety ... with an attitude," she added. Annie Peavey nodded her approval.

"M' mama gib me dis fo she got solt," said Annie indicating the bracelet made from an intricate twist of knots of fabric that she wore around her wrist.

Piper, whose silence, despite his muscular build, made him easy to ignore, seemed more interested in Rheena than in what she was wearing. And while the girls spoke, his intense eyes studied her, looking to the ground at their feet or to a place off to the side whenever Rheena looked in his direction.

"They sold your mother?" Rheena asked. Annie made no reply but asked a question of her own.

"Tweety, is you a haint?"

"I told you!" Zachary laughed again.

"My name is not Tweety. It's Rheena. And I'm no ghost either," she said jutting her chin forward as if to dare a rebuttal. Without warning, Piper raised his hand and poked Rheena hard in the arm with a stick that had been concealed by his side.

"Ow!" Rheena yelped. She tugged at her sleeve, scrubbing the sudden pain with her knuckles. A tiny spot of blood appeared and trickled down her arm to stain her blouse.

"That hurt!" she complained.

Piper examined the wound with his fingertip.

"Flesh 'n blood," Piper muttered. Satisfied, he turned and walked away.

Annie studied the spot on Rheena's arm then turned to follow after Piper. Rheena and Zachary stood stunned as they watched them leave.

"Wait!" Rheena called after a moment. Then she and Zachary raced to catch up with their new friends.

In silence, Piper strolled off into the woods, the three not far behind him. With the skill that comes with habit, he picked his way through the brush, stepping with ease over fallen branches and rocks that jutted out of the ground. After a short walk the earth became soft and mushy under their feet. When Rheena saw that Annie had begun to pick up twigs and bundled them in her arms, she joined in. Annie Peavey seemed to be selective in her choice of branches and twigs, while Rheena looked for the pieces of wood that weren't going to get her clothes too messy.

Piper and Zachary soon vanished amongst the white oak trees up ahead. Before she tired from the walk, the trees gave way to open air, and Rheena and Annie stepped out into a clearing where water splashed against the rocks that lined the bank of a narrow stream.

"Look!" Zachary yelled as the two girls walked toward him. "We found a cootah!"

Zachary and Piper held either end of the shell of a large turtle. Its head swung limp as did it flippers.

"Piper wunked it real hard over the head with a rock," The enthusiasm in his voice brimmed with pride. "Look at it! I'm not even scared."

He and Piper flipped the turtle onto its shell and propped the tail end up with a few rocks. The turtle's head lulled to one side. It was dead. Rheena looked at her brother Zachary anticipating his revulsion would match her own; however, he was fascinated by the creature that moments earlier ambled along the shore of the river but now lay belly up on its shell.

Piper produced a knife from his waist belt and with some effort, cut off the turtle's head. Rheena dropped her bundle of sticks to the ground and stepped back from the carnage. Determining that this was as good a spot as any Annie also dropped her bundle of sticks and set about shaping them into what soon became the location for a campfire. Rheena watched with disgust as Piper made a careful slit down the underbelly of the turtle, exposing entrails and gore. The liquid and blood from the turtle pooled in tiny rivulets on the ground.

Piper gripped the knife as he squatted beside the amphibian, cutting through tendons and sinew, slicing meaty pieces of turtle flesh into chunks. He picked discriminately through the gory content of the shell discarding some of it into a hole in the soft earth that he had dug with his knife.

Satisfied with his work, Piper produced from his rucksack several stubby carrots, a fat, round potato and a large yellow onion. He cut these roots into pieces and dropped them into the shell. Rheena joined

Zachary and Annie who gathered cupped hands full of stream water to spill into the shell that now rested on their open fire.

While dinner cooked, the four scoured up and down the riverbank and into the thickets to gather the blackberries, raspberries, dewberries, wine-berries, chickweed and wintercress that grew there in abundance. The potherbs that didn't go into the rucksacks joined the vegetables in the turtle shell. The berries became juicy snacks that they stuffed into their mouths or tucked into the sacks to be later sorted for jam by Aint Zori.

Rheena followed Zachary and Annie who ventured away from the open fire to forage deeper into the marsh swamp land.

"Don' step dere!" Annie Peavy shouted the warning as she grabbed Zachary's arm and yanked him backward and onto the ground. "Morass suck you down!" Annie Peavey cried.

"Morass?" Rheena asked as she hurried over to help her brother to his feet. They eased back away from the swampy wet ground.

"Qwik-san!" Piper said from a short distance away. He joined them and helped them pull their feet from the sticky wet earth.

"Quicksand?" Rheena echoed in horror, grateful for Annie Peavey's swift intervention.

Piper held Zachary by the arm until the boy was sure of his footing. Annie Peavey retraced their steps out of the marshy tangle of grass that was now underfoot. Now and again Piper took Annie's carry sack as she grabbled over a difficult spot so as not to disturb its content. He lifted Rheena up and over a spot that had been easy to cross in the coming in but not so in the going out. The ground made sucking sounds underfoot as they made their way, stepping up high and pulling on branches for leverage, back to the clearing. Their retreat was slow and cautious as Piper led them to safety. At long last, the ground was solid beneath their feet. It was then that they ventured a glance back toward the swampy marsh that had almost claimed Zachary.

"Nut'n dat way seppin' gators 'n slow deaf," Piper said matter-of-factly as he led them toward their Sunday dinner by the water's edge.

The two children felt secure in the company of the teenagers. Neither in Brooklyn nor in Monticello would any of Hoban's friends have tolerated Rheena or Zachary as these two did. No pranks. No hiding or leaping from dark places. Here was Piper and Annie Peavey spending time with Rheena and Zachary despite the difference in their age.

"We have a brother, you know," said Rheena. She thought now of Hoban as they walked in silence, their breathing blending in with the other sounds of nature around them. She missed Hoban and home deeply.

"I bet you and him are the same age," she offered.

In her mind, Rheena compared Hoban's strength and cleverness to that of Piper. "His name is Hoban. He's smart. But he gets into trouble a lot. He knows karate." She pronounced it *car-rot-tay* so her audience would be sure to understand its importance.

"Sometimes he calls me names." Rheena complained one moment, reminisced the next. "I don't like it when he does that! But

I call him names back." Annie nodded. Rheena looked down at the ground as they walked.

"We used to live in Brooklyn. There wasn't a lotta dirt like here. Dirt and trees and stuff like that. Mostly sidewalks. And tall buildings."

She remembered their brownstone on Macon Street where she and Zachary, Hoban and Mama had lived most of her life. In her mind, she ran up the three flights of stairs to their apartment. The place in her memory was filled with the boxes that contained their belongings. In her mind, she could only find the last day there.

"We had a stoop." She thought a moment and amended her statement. "That's the same as saying steps. Only more."

She spoke as they walked about Brooklyn and its busy streets. People going to places and coming from places, then disappearing inside. She herself hadn't played outside much. Some of the other children did, not her and Zachary though. Too many cars and buses and thing that can get you in trouble Mama warned. So she mostly sat on that stoop she'd just described to Annie and Piper, who listened with polite fascination to the words that held no meaning for them.

Sometimes, Rheena continued, she and the other kids would jump off the stoop. The one who could jump from the top step to the wrought iron gate at the bottom, without falling on the ground, was the winner. Since no children her age lived in their building, that game was only enjoyed when the children from across the street came over to play. She drew chalk pictures and hopscotch grids on the sidewalk. She did play outside at school during recess: dodgeball, monkey in the middle, double-Dutch, relay. She was a fast runner, she told them.

Rheena told her audience about crowded shopping.

"We went downtown to shop, especially for back to school. We hardly ever took the car. No place to park. We rode the bus. Sometimes we rode the train into Manhattan. We didn't do that much, though, because we would have to carry our packages back on the subway. *What a nightmare,* Mama always complained, about the parking and the subway ride!" Zachary nodded.

"Then we moved." Her reverie deepened. "We always visited Papa in the summer time. Now, that's where we live all the time. Until now," she added.

Annie Peavey and Piper listened as Rheena droned on in what sounded to them like a foreign language. Even Zachary listened.

"My mama's name is Shirley, Shirley Mackey," she continued.

"I don't know my mama."

Piper broke his silence when Rheena mentioned Shirley. He shrugged his shoulders when Zachary said:

"That's so sad."

Had they not been in this precarious and confusing situation, Rheena might have enjoyed their Sunday morning outing with Piper and Annie Peavey. Talking about Mama and Hoban warmed her heart. Somehow the talking made her feel less hopeless. Papa always said fresh air could *clear d' mind.* Yet, their walking now only cluttered her mind. In school her teachers always said *use your five Ws!* However, here, she only knew three of the Ws. She knew no more about the *what* or the *why* of her and Zachary's predicament. If they were to get back home to Mama and Hoban and Papa's burned down house, they would need all of the *W*s, as well as, the *how*.

When the four was securely back at their campfire, they sat on the ground and ate the turtle stew in silence. Each dipped wooden spoons and chunks of bread into the inverted shell and ravenously slurped the content.

Despite her muddled thoughts and the clutter in her head, Rheena considered how peaceful it was here. The sun, which was not yet full up in the sky, warmed them. The backwater relaxed them. Their surroundings, calm and quiet, except for the sporadic splash of the black crappies who fed on the abundant mayfly nymphs. It was serene at this part of the river, not quite reached by the current, where the water stood stagnant. And it was peaceful. It was tranquil.

That is until they heard the shrill scream that pierced through their Sunday morning reverie. The high-pitched screech ripped through their silence like a giant piece of Styrofoam being torn from a packing box.

The shriek terrified the four with its sudden and frightening other worldliness. The chilling cry emanated from out of the swamp. As one, they bolted upright. Rheena grasped Zachary's arm in terror knocking the wooden spoon filled with bits of potato and carrot from his hand. Piper grabbed the knife that earlier served him as a cooking tool, then a shovel. Now he held it for its intended purpose, a weapon. He crouched pantherlike beside the fire and stared into the gloomy mist that roiled across the murky landscape on the far side of the river.

"What was that!" Rheena whispered. She gripped her little brother for both protection and comfort, as she tried desperately to peer through the fog of darkness across the water. Her heart pounded in her chest

"It be da win'," said Annie Peavy, uncertainty coloring her whispered words.

"Don' be no win'," Piper corrected.

His gaze was fixed on the other side of the river. Zachary pulled himself from Rheena's tight grip in order to slip closer to where Piper crouched, brave and panther like. All the while his head lowered, he too stared through hooded eyes across the water.

"No!" Piper cautioned.

He threw his arm in front of the energetic boy keeping him back from harm's way. The quartet remained at alert for untold heartbeats. Waiting. But nothing more followed the bone chilling sound they had just experienced.

Their meal was done.

They gathered up their bounty of river roots, potherbs, wild-berries and fish. Piper snuffed the fire with his foot, and they headed back to the quarters leaving behind the river, the tall grasses, and the solitude. They never noticed, as they made their way through the dense woods, from across the river, someone watched them.

11

Maroons

RED GATHERED UP the provisions he had procured with the help of the strange new arrival. He added to these stores four fresh killed chickens, two live chickens and as many vegetables as he could stuff into his ruck sacks. The birds, live and dead, hung upside down by a twist of cord wrapped around their legs and draped across his shoulders. The eggs he secured in cloth; the roots he crammed in on top of them.

When he was certain the plantation Blacks were otherwise engaged in off-day activities the Badger slipped off unnoticed into the woods. He headed back into the community of Maroons, the outliers who for more than a century survived in the harsh conditions of the swamp rather than endure the harsh conditions of servitude.

With him Red carried essential food stores that swamp life was hard pressed to provide -- flour, salt, bread, dried beans, fresh chicken, eggs, to name a few. He traded or bartered hogs, alligator and other meats from hunting. Red also carried news to the maroons from the world outside the swamp. They depended on him for that, just as the plantation depended on the resourcefulness of the Maroons. The enslaved on the Hammond Plantation as well as the maroons who lived in the swamp, relied on him. This day it was the news of the two new arrivals that materialized out of the nothingness much as Mama Bayou had predicted when he was a child.

The going was not easy laden as he was; however, the way was familiar; and the Badger was equally at home in the swamps as on the plantation. Countless times Red, as he was aptly named on account of the orange and red naps of hair on the top of his head, on his chin, around his mouth and up and down his arms and legs, splashed through these swamps, tromped through the brackish waters. As he traveled, he pulled common reeds aside, sometimes even swam, in order to get to the community of maroons.

After a short stride, the sounds of the melodic patter of Sunday on the plantation was replaced by the chirps, belches and grunts that was the swamp. The uneven clay and dirt underfoot soon gave way to the mucky decayed vegetation surrounding shoulder-high cattails. Invasive phragmites shot up all around him forcing Red to lift the bundles he carried high overhead to keep them dry.

A few feet away from where the Badger waded, eyes floated at the surface of the murky water. He watched them just as they watched him. Red knew that, typically, swamp alligators fed at dusk or at dawn. They avoided humans as much as humans needed to avoid them; however, a man-size meal can be enticing to a hungry 'gator this time of the morning. Red's agile fingers began to detangle the cord from around the legs of one of the chickens suspended at his neck. The bird began to stir.

"It be u o' it be me, bird," the Badger crooned.

He flung the squawking fowl out over the expanse of water. An alligator exploded, open mouth, out of the water leaping more than its length into the air. In one snap of powerful jaws the chicken was gone. Before the reptile could land in the water, the Badger tossed a second shrieking chicken flying into the air. The alligator back flipped to snatch the fowl out of the air before crashing back down into the water. The alligator swallowed its chicken meal. The water roiled under Red's feet as he struggled to the relative safety of drier land.

Red walked about an hour more before the mounds of earth appeared through the cane breaks. The handful of people who lived here made their homes in dugouts. Mama Bayou's house, the only true structure, stood back farther from the other dwellings.

Made of wooden planks and fallen trees, some stacked horizontally, some vertically, the abode leaned precariously to the right where a wall of burlap sacks seamed together, provided minimal support. The shanty had no windows, and the roof was balanced on top as if as a necessary afterthought. There was one doorless opening. Red entered Mama Bayou's home.

The ageless Black woman squatted in the center of the single room strumming her fingers through the bits of cloth on the ground in front of her. She showed neither surprise or pleasure at his arrival and continued the unclear task set before her.

"Mama." Red greeted Mama Bayou with fondness and great respect.

He dropped the provisions he'd brought onto the board that served as a table. He spread out each sack letting enough of the content spill out for easy identification. The remaining three chickens plopped down beside the dried goods.

"Red. Wha u brung?" Mama Bayou croaked. She pulled her slight frame from the ground with more facility than expected and strode around the table. Her hands floated leisurely above the items there as if in blessing. The Badger watched, solemn and humbled. He was eager to share the rest of what he carried.

The swamp woman rarely spoke and the few words she uttered scraped across vocal cords as old and as dry as she. She turned her face toward the ceiling, placed both hands on either side of her mouth and howled. Red gritted his teeth and plugged his ears with his fingertips. It was a ghostly wail. It came from deep within the bowels of the ancestors. The single tone, sustained and unrelenting, undulated through the swamp, across the streams and to the Hammond Plantations. Many who heard thought it to be the wind. Others believed it to be the spectral call of a long-gone soul. Some pretended they did not hear it. Others indeed did not hear it.

Outside Mama Bayou's shanty house, the swamp people who refused plantation life began to gather. They brought goods of their own for trade and barter. Chunks of alligator meat, whole and skinned rabbit, crawdad and cray fish, black and white crappie, frogs, and wild pig all joined the Badger's flour, beans, cornmeal, eggs, chicken, and indigo. Systematically, they gathered up Red's bounty, added it to the other merchandise and set up shop outside the shanty.

Carrots and potatoes of varying colors, shapes and sizes filled straw baskets beside baskets of leeks and mounds of parsnips. Chard, spinach, mustard, and collard greens fanned on a board next to red, green and yellow peppers. Animal fur and animal skin splayed on the ground next to tubs of lard and licks of salt. Tiny tins of ointments and salves were stacked on makeshift shelves next to brown and green bottles of elixirs and liniments. Chickens skittered underfoot, some bare, some booted. Before long, the open-air market bustled with maroons, outliers and slavery's other exiles who had made their home in the swamp. They traded and bartered, haggled, and negotiated before retreating into the marshland.

"Mama Bayou, I brung u tidin's," the Badger said after he had secured his own provisions. He moved back into the shanty house and squatted on the ground by her side. Mama Bayou leaned back in the worn-out cane chair Red had brought through the swamp years ago.

"I din' see it from d' start. But I seed it at d' finish," he began as a disclaimer. "We all hear'd the thunder and the bangin'. Hear'd jus' as clear as ya' wanna be. Black fok c'mence t' runnin' t' d' qua'tas," he said dramatically. "Time I be there … had awready happin'!" the Badger added with more than a hint of disappointment in his voice. "Two pik'a'ninnies jus' be a dancin' an' a bangin' like the ole ways!"

He stopped his narrative as he recalled the morning of the day before. His head bobbing slowly as if to convince himself of the validity of the event.

"I hear'd dat drummin'," Mama Bayou said affirming the Badgers tale.

"Brownridge, scoop 'um right away 'n thow'd 'em inna Aint Zori's."

"Humph!" was all Mama Bayou said.

"Thow'd da drum right 'n wit' 'em," he continued.

"Humph!" she added.

"Dat gal wha' hep me wit' alla dis' hea'," he said indicating the organized chaos going on outside the shanty around the provisions.

"She hep'yu'?"

"Jes' as bol' as yu' pleez!" The Badger began to pace inside the shanty. There wasn't much to the space; the table and the chair where Mama Bayou sat dominated. A bed fashioned out of rice chaff and cloths lay on the floor at the wall. Pots and skillets, bowls and cooking utensils of various materials, shapes and sizes were heaped on the floor in the corner by the door. Just outside the doorway, the river rocks piled in a circle served for cooking.

"Humph," was all that Mama Bayou said.

The Badger needed to give Mama Bayou the rest of what he had carried from the Hammond Plantation. He hadn't seen the two appear; nevertheless, the telling of their arrival had come from so many of the slaves. Some of them he knew to be liars. Many told tales and he knew there was great exaggeration in their stories. Others of them he had learned to trust for the truth. Red only brought Mama Bayou truths because she was a seer and could see in many directions, backward and forward, upward and downward, events in the past and things yet to come to pass. She could see long, and she could see far. He would only tell her what he himself had heard, what he himself had seen.

First there was the horrifying, earsplitting thunder. That he heard. Then, there was the drums. The vicious sound of many drums pounding all at once. He heard the drumming that was strictly forbidden and had been for a very long time: the drumming out of Africa. That, he heard. He told how he pulled himself up from the dirt where he had fallen; how he ran like the others to the Quarters to see what he was hearing; how he had to shove his way through the crowd that had already gathered.

He told the far seer how he himself saw the two children. Through the dust and the dirt and the sparks, he saw the dancer girl and the drummer boy. Their hands and feet and arms flailing to the rhythms of Africa. Too much sound for just the two pickaninnies to be making; but that was what he saw and that was what he heard. That is what he told Mama Bayou. When the two who had appeared out of the nothingness stopped their movement and fell to the ground Africa stopped too. These were the tidings he brought to the molly-gassa woman, Mama Bayou.

He knew she listened. Even though he told his story as he stared out the door into the distance, he knew she listened. The barterers and the traders listened. They had heard it; however, he had seen it.

"Humph!"

"Dat' not da whol' uv it," the Badger said as he turned to Mama Bayou. "D' gal kin sai'fa!"

For the first time since the Badger began his telling of the day before, the old swamp woman looked at him.

"She sai'fas?" she whispered.

"Yah'sem. I seed dat too!" he said. "In da stores," he added. "She ope up massa Orrie's brown ledja book an' run ha li'l finga long massa Orrie's scrachin's like she know'd zak'ly wha' dem scrachin's mean."

"Humph," the sound this time barely a puff of air from her nostrils.

There was a long silence before either spoke again. It was Mama Bayou who broke the quiet.

"*Ankey dje, anke be*" she muttered in the old tongue of the Yoruba people; "Eva'one gather t'gether." she translated to no one in particular. She took a deep breath and exhaled a long sigh. "It be so long, cullit folks forgets. It been beat outta us. Red, yu say you hear'd many drums but only see'd one drum?"

The Badger nodded.

"Der be three spirits in da drum." Mama Bayou began. "Der be da spirit a da tree dat gibs da wood fo' da drum. Den d'ey be spirit a da animal wha' skin is used fo' da drumhead. Las', the may'ka ov da drum fills da drum wit d'ey spirit. Talk 'bout da spirits ov da ancestors. OooWee!" she exclaimed. "Mos' pow'ful!"

He nodded his head to the affirmative, but he didn't understand.

"Ancestors sen' dem chi'ren."

"Wha' fo'?" he asked.

There was no comprehension in him. From his childhood to this moment, Red had only known the life between the swamp and the plantation. Eating, sleeping, thieving, and hiding; hunting and trading was all he ever did. There had never been play or rice crops or beatings. None of that had ever been his lot.

"She be owa t'morrow," Mama Bayou repeated patiently. "She be owa few-cha'," her voice hoarse from nonuse.

The Badger nodded duly and listened.

"You keep yo eye on dem chi'ren!" Mama Bayou lifted two gnarly fingers to her eye then pointed them at him. This he understood. "You go tell Aint Zori and dat Brownridge t' keep dem chi'ren safe! Keep 'em safe! Dey be ow few-cha!"

Mama Bayou fell again into silence. Red grabbed up the wild hog's head, the rabbit meat, and the chunks of alligator meat that had been set aside for him, and he left. He made his way back through the marshy swamp to the shallow bank of the river.

"*You keep an eye on them chi'ren!*" the old conjurer woman Mama Bayou had warned him. And that is exactly what he did. Shrouded in the mist and the tall bullrush, Red squatted at the water's edge and watched. An alert Piper crouched on the far side, a protective arm shielding the boy, as he strained to see across the water and into the fog. Nevertheless, Red was confident that he was not seen by the clever young slave or by Annie Peavy who coward next to the girl.

He watched the four kick out their fire and gather up their belongings then turn in the direction of the plantation. Had they dared to looked back to the river, they would have noticed the Badger as he slipped out of the fog and into the water. With his provisions held high above his head, he waded silently to dry land. However, they never looked back so did not see him follow them back to the quarters.

About the author

TR FARONII is a Brooklyn born, native New Yorker. An interest in music, writing, and communication fueled an early career on stage, screen, and television. She writes short stories, articles and has written several plays, including *Dixie Peach and Wolf Reads: The Musical*. In addition to teaching English at the college level, Faronii, works with at risk youths and individuals with learning and developmental differences. An independent bookseller, The Way Maker young adult series is her debut as a novelist.

Acknowledgements

A SPECIAL THANKS must go to all the way makers who have gone before me to make a way out of no way.

Thank you, my soul sister Sandy Avery-Nubian, who offered endless encouragement and support as I wrote throughout the years. To my editor, Christopher Mele, who combed through each word, comma, period, and quotation mark before telling me I had "a tiger by the tail."

To my cover artist Jacquelyn Bynum who could see it.

To my children Kel, Reliina, Bell and Tae, the loves of my life and constant inspiration to me, who are making a way for my beloved grandchildren and for so many others. To my companion who has been patient even as he makes his own journey to freedom. Thank you to my two sisters Jeanette and Ornyece who still walk with me.

Special thanks must go to my beta-readers Jacques Laine, Valerie Bynum, and G. Oliver King, as well as, to the members of the Greater Lehigh Valley Writers Group.

Thank you, Mother and Daddy. I am eternally grateful.

Keep a look out for book two

There We Have it

in *the Way Makers* series by T.R. Faronii
Follow Rheena, Zachary and their big brother Hoban on their

Journey to Freedom

Coming soon!

www.ingramcontent.com/pod-product-compliance
Lightning Source LLC
LaVergne TN
LVHW011839060526
838200LV00054B/4095